THE FRIENDSTONE

by Martha Derman

Publication Date: April 1980
Price: $8.95; $8.44 library edition
Fiction
Ages 9-12 years   Grades 4-7
160 pages
ISBN: 0-8037-2472-1; -2480-2 library edition

Eleven-year-old Sally Moffat thought she'd
go mad with boredom. In the summer of 1929,
recovering from whooping cough in Pleasanton,
New York, there is just <u>nothing</u> to do. So
when Aunt Samantha invites Sally for a visit
to the Catskill Mountains, she is overjoyed.
     Right after she arrives, she meets
Evie Grauber, who is staying at Grossman's
Hotel. Evie seems agressive and grabby.
At first Sally can't stand her. But guided
by her great-grandmother's generosity, she
begins to enjoy Evie's company and to dis-
cover the pleasures of a life tantalizingly
different from her own. Later on when Sally's
summer ends in tragedy, Evie is the one
who best understands her loss.
     In this rich and subtle novel, set
against the background of an earlier era,
Martha Derman traces the progress of an un-
expected and most valuable friendship.

Martha Derman grew up on the East Coast and spent her teen-age years in the San Francisco-Bay Area. She received her Master's degree in library science from Columbia University. An avid traveler, she has lived in Austria, Great Britain, Israel, and Italy, and currently resides in Chappaqua, New York, with her husband and two children.

Ms. Derman has been writing since she was ten years old. This is her first novel, and she has already begun work on a second.

THE FRIENDSTONE

Martha Derman

The Dial Press / New York

Printed in the United States of America

First Printing

Library of Congress Cataloging in Publication
Data

Derman, Martha.
    The friendstone.

    SUMMARY: Eleven-year-old Sally's view
of life expands when she becomes friends
with a Jewish girl the summer of 1929,
which she spends in the Catskills with
her beloved grandmother.
    [1.   Jews in the United States--Fiction.
2.   Grandmothers--Fiction.   3.   Death--
Fiction.   I.   Title.
PZ7.D44Fr   [Fic]   80-24711
ISBN 0-8037-2472-1
ISBN 0-8037-2480-2 (lib. bdg.)

THE FRIENDSTONE

Martha Derman

The Dial Press / New York

Printed in the United States of America

First Printing

Library of Congress Cataloging in Publication
Data

Derman, Martha.
    The friendstone.

    SUMMARY: Eleven-year-old Sally's view
of life expands when she becomes friends
with a Jewish girl the summer of 1929,
which she spends in the Catskills with
her beloved grandmother.
    [1.   Jews in the United States--Fiction.
2.   Grandmothers--Fiction.   3.   Death--
Fiction.   I.   Title.
PZ7.D44Fr   [Fic]   80-24711
ISBN 0-8037-2472-1
ISBN 0-8037-2480-2   (lib. bdg.)

THE FRIENDSTONE

Chapter I

Sally sat on her wide front porch and picked her nose. She did it out of utter boredom, and because she knew her neat, clean, crisp mother hated her to do it. Sally imagined her mother's voice: What will the neighbors think? Sally was sick and tired of that particular phrase.

Trouble was, she *was* sick. Sort of. In Pleasanton, New York, July 1929, there was a lot of whooping cough, and Sally and her two brothers, Sam and Colin, all had it. Sally experimented with a cough, to see if a real whoop lay underneath. She waited, finger poised at one nostril. No, she was not going to have a big whoop at the moment. Good. She could stay and watch Steve Baer, on his porch across the street, play his banjo. There was another boy with him. Sally stopped poking at her nose and hoped they were going to play and sing together. Since Steve had got home from college, at the beginning of the month, there had been an ongoing party on the Baers' front porch. Sally liked to hear the group of freshmen play their banjos and ukuleles. It was a bright spot in her awful summer.

Since the middle of June, when the doctor had told Mrs. Moffat that Sally, Sam, and Colin had whooping cough, there had been nothing to do except watch and listen to Steve Baer and his friends, count the Pierce-Arrows and the Paiges on Hamilton Street, and cough. When Sally coughed, she lost her breath and gasped for air, like a fish out of water. It was like drowning in a sea of coughs, every wave a whoop.

Sally was supposed to "play quietly" that summer of 1929. She played interminable games of checkers, cards, and anagrams with Sam, and a stupid Uncle Wiggly game with Colin, who was only a first grader. Their father pitched an old Army tent in the backyard, and the three of them camped out. But as soon as they realized "camping out" meant resting on canvas cots in a hot tent—Mrs. Moffat's way of keeping them quiet—the game became very dull.

That morning, when Steve Baer left in his friend's Model-T Ford, Sally went inside and wound up the Victrola. She was just about to start dancing to the music when Colin came running in and scraped the phonograph arm over the grooves. "There's a parade outside Sal," he yelled. "Horses and everything. Come and see."

Then Sally caught the drums throbbing in the air. A parade, in the middle of such a grim summer, was a miracle. She bounded onto the porch and sat down. Sam was already on the steps, hunched next to Plush, their cocker spaniel. He had an arm around the dog's neck because you had to keep him from following parades.

"Lookit," whispered Colin, "everybody's Halloween spooks."

They were. The drummers—and the band was only drums, dozens and dozens of them—were dressed like ghosts, with peaked heads. Sally felt the boom of the drums vibrate in the very pit of her stomach. She was awed by the mass of draped figures. She could see black shoes and trouser cuffs at the hems of the white robes, but there were no faces, only eyeholes in the sheets. Occasionally the holes flashed. Sally knew there must be real men under there and that some of them wore eyeglasses that winked in the sunshine. Between the slow beats of the drums, she could hear the shuffle of feet on pavement. No one shouted or gave directions. Sally's skin crawled. "What are they?" she breathed, afraid to speak out loud. Her mother stepped out the door, but did not answer.

"What've they done to those horses?" Sam whispered. His voice croaked, almost husky with dismay. Behind the marching men was a platoon of riders on dark chestnuts. The riders were cloaked and hooded like the walkers and drummers. The horses' hooves were muffled,

3

tied into canvas sacks. You could tell the horses did not like wearing the sacks. Though they were reined in tight to walk slowly, several snorted and showed the whites of their eyes. They gave sidling steps along the asphalt and bunched their sleek rumps nervously. One horse reared on his hind legs, but the rider did not even say, "Whoa."

As the masked riders came even with the Moffats' front yard, Colin yelled, "Hurrah," and leaped to the sidewalk.

At his shout, Mrs. Moffat came awake. She grabbed Colin by the waist of his button-on shorts and shooed the three of them inside. "You can watch from the windows," she said. "Don't smudge the glass." She leaned over their shoulders to see too.

The horses disappeared up Hamilton Street. Several more marchers came into view, carrying a street-wide pennant. It was so big it took a dozen men to hold it aloft with poles and golden ropes. The pennant was beautiful, of purple satin, with golden fringe. Sam read it aloud: " 'K—K—K. Order of the Grand Dragon.' What's that mean?" he said.

"Ku Klux Klan." Mrs. Moffat drew her lips into a thin line. Sally thought her mother looked troubled. A spattering of applause came from people who had gathered on porches and sidewalks. The Moffats could hear it through the open door. One rider, on the biggest, blackest horse Sally had ever seen, dominated the street. The applause was for him. He rode alone, followed by two horseman who each carried a purple-and-gold flag. Even the canvas on the horses' hooves was purple. Colin started to clap.

Though they were inside, Mrs. Moffat folded his hands into hers so that he made no sound. "Why can't I clap?" Colin stared at his mother through tangles of uncut hair. None of them, of course, had been near a barber for a month. "Those people outside are clapping."

Mrs. Moffat only shook her head. "That's the end," she said. "Some limousines of bigwigs to bring up the rear. People who don't ride horses, I suppose. Come now, and I'll play hearts with you till it's time to get dinner."

"I want to know about the parade," said Sam. At eight, Sam had to have answers instantly. "Don't you know who they are either? Why can't we clap?"

"I told you. It's the Ku Klux Klan. And not everybody applauded, only a few. I don't think—well, what would the neighbors think if I let you clap for a controversial group like that?"

"Controversial?" said Sally.

"Oh, it's all *political*," said her mother. Sally noted her mother's disparaging tone of voice. "I don't want to think about them anymore. Ask your father. Get the cards."

All through the game of hearts, Sally mulled over the canvas-covered hooves and the silent marchers. She could hardly wait to ask her father when he came home for dinner. "What's the Ku Klux Klan?" she said while Sam yelled about horses, and Colin tried to explain the costumes.

"One at a time," said Mr. Moffat. "I'd heard the Klan was going to march. So they came by here, huh? Maybe they want to give old Baer something to think about." He chuckled.

"What do you mean?" asked Sally. "What *would* Mr. Baer think about?"

Her father laughed and rumpled Sally's hair. "My eleven-year-old Rapunzel," he said, "with hair long enough to braid. It's nice you're letting it grow."

Sally drew her hair out of her father's grasp. He knew a short bob was the style as well as she did. She was tired of jokes. "Nobody ever answers me," she said. She coughed. She was tired of coughing. "Ma said it's political. You say they marched to make Mr. Baer think. Honestly, nobody's really thinking because nobody makes sense."

"Nothing to worry about," said her father. "The KKK *is* kind of political. The main thing is they're out to discourage foreigners from grabbing too big a hunk of American enterprise."

"The Baers are American."

"Ye-e-e-ess." Mr. Moffat kind of drawled the word. "But they're Jews. In the North the Klan doesn't encourage Jews."

"Does it encourage them in the South?" asked Sally.

Mr. Moffat cleared his throat. "Well, of course, you know in the South, the Klan's been around a long time to give the uppity colored what for. Negroes, I mean; the

6

Klan's kept them in their place."

"What place is that?" Sally said. Negroes, Sally knew from school, had been slaves before the Civil War, but the Emancipation Proclamation had given them their freedom. Her history book had a picture of Abraham Lincoln writing it.

"Come on now, you don't want—that is—" Her father began to sound irritable. "Never mind the South, let's stick to *here*, kiddo. The Klan's out to protect business. American business. They want to save it from, uh, from oh, the Irish catholics, the Negroes, or the Jews, uh well, the foreigners, see."

Sally asked, "Which business, Daddy, the buying part, or the selling part, or the making part?"

"See here!" Uh-oh, now her father was mad. Sally could tell. His face was flushed and his eyes seemed cold. "Who the heck you think you're grilling? I didn't say *I* thought these things. I'm trying to tell you about the *Klan*. Maybe foreigners aren't good for business. They undercut everyone else. They sell lower, work for less. They demean a neighborhood."

Sally understood her father was interested in business all right. He read the stock pages in the newspaper every day and predicted he was going to make a killing. He said times were right for it, and that everybody was making money hand over fist. Once, earlier in the summer, he had joked that he wished he had a dollar for every whoop Sally, Sam, and Colin coughed so he'd be a millionaire. "But *what* isn't good for business?" Sally persisted. "The Baers have a big garage downtown—that's a business. I don't understand why you . . ."

"Hush. Never mind," her mother broke in. "It's too complicated for you. Stop thinking so much and help me set the table."

"I *like* to think," said Sally. She was cross. She caught a glimpse of her frown in the mirror of the sideboard and frowned even deeper.

She was very dissatisfied with herself this summer. It wasn't only the lankiness of her blond hair. It was everything. She'd grown quite tall and skinny. It seemed to her that her blue eyes had faded, her nose had grown sharper, her freckles had paled to the point of disappearing. She'd had no friends, no camp adventures, nothing exciting except a parade that was scary; and now her father and mother were talking in puzzles. She could see it now: When school opened in September, some teacher was going to require an English theme, "How I Spent My Summer Vacation," and Sally Moffat could write it in one sentence. "I spent my vacation coughing and wondering what the neighbors' business was." It was a rotten vacation, that's what. "It really stinks," Sally said, but no one was around to hear.

Chapter II

Then on Tuesday morning Aunt Samantha's letter arrived. Mr. McDougal, the regular postman, slipped it through the mail slot in the front door with the usual *click-clack*. But once it was opened, that letter came into Sally's summer like a freight train hooting *FFFRREEE-DOM.*

Aunt Samantha lived in the Catskill Mountains, year round, in a village called Cottersville. Every summer Sally and her family spent two weeks at Aunt Samantha's, and Sally loved the mountains. Having heard about the progress of ailing Moffat children, Aunt Samantha now wrote to invite Sally for a visit. "By myself?" asked Sally. No Sam, no Colin. No mother or father! She danced around the living room and hugged herself while her mother read bits of Aunt Samantha's letter aloud.

Mrs. Moffat pursed her lips at Sally. "Careful. When you get excited, you bring on the coughing. Easy now." Sally sat on the piano bench but gave hops and shifts of excitement.

"Read some more," she said. "I'll be quiet."

" 'We have been thinking you must need some relief from sick children, Marcia [that was Ma], and that Sally is quite old enough to visit by herself for a few weeks.' "

"Golly yes!" Sally put her hand over her mouth.

"You keep interrupting, I can't read 'You and the boys can come later, when they're well. Is Sally well enough to come on Saturday? Packer says [that was Uncle Packer Mead, Aunt Samantha's second husband and very nice] that he will look after Sally while I am in the shop.' "

"What about Grandma? What does she say about Grandma?" Great-grandmother Byrd lived with the Meads. She was the one amazing grown-up in Sally's life, because she was connected with nothing but pure joy. Much as Sally loved Aunt Samantha and Uncle Packer, for Grandmother Byrd she experienced a feeling so special that it was almost beyond putting into words, even to herself. "What about Grandma?"

"Um," said her mother. She read along. " 'I am busy at the shop, and your grandmother is looking forward to having some life around here. She says Packer and I are

10

getting too old for her.'" Sally giggled. Aunt Samantha was only a little older than her father, though she was really his aunt and Sally's great-aunt. "Grandma" was a true great-grandmother and eighty-two years old.

Mrs. Moffat considered Sally, who was diddling her fingers over the piano keys. "Sally, you dream so much, even when you're wide awake. You're certainly well enough to go now. Can you behave yourself? You've never been there alone before."

"Pretty please with sugar on it." Sally stopped fidgeting and willed herself to be calm. To have Aunt Samantha's to herself, Grandma to herself, were unimagined treats. Besides, she'd have all of the cottage for her own explorations.

"You must remember to pick up your clothes, Sally. Lord knows I've been trying to get you to know when your underwear needs washing. You'll have to wash your own socks and not leave them for Grandmother Byrd."

"Of course," said Sally. "I like making lots of suds."

"That's *just* it!" said Mrs. Moffat. "You *play* at everything. You'll have soapsuds lathering the entire bathroom. The way you wash your hair, you'd think soap grew on trees."

Sally's eyes widened. Hey, what a keen idea, a soap tree with bubbles for leaves.

"And you don't pay attention to your elders, Sally. It is a very bad habit."

Oh, yes, pay attention. Sally focused on her mother's face. Ma was so pretty, really, with light-brown curly hair. Everything about her was round and soft and curvy. Everything about Sally was long and straight and skinny. She wished she looked more like her mother instead of like herself.

Mrs. Moffat finished saying something and rattled the pages of the letter. Then she gazed out the window. "Don't you think so?" she said.

Oops. What was it Sally was supposed to be thinking about? "Yes," she said and kept a serious face. It seemed to satisfy her mother. Boy, that was a close one. You had to watch your step with parents. Mentally, Sally gave a little prayer: God, if you'll let me go to Aunt Samantha's, I'll—I'll make my bed the proper way every single morning. That was a hard promise. She hated to take time to smooth the sheets and pull the spread tight. God, I *will*, I swear I really will, forever and ever, world without end, A-a-amen. She moved her lips as if she were singing in Sunday school.

Mrs. Moffat turned to look at her. "What did you say?" Sally shook her head and lowered her eyes. She folded her hands in her lap and simply thought to God: Please.

Mrs. Moffat narrowed her eyes at her daughter. Sally held her breath in case she was pulsating excitement into the stuffy living room. "You must remember to listen, to mind your P's and Q's. You've gotten so dreamy, I wonder if you'll remember to get your clothes on right side out. Keep that long hair combed."

"Ma, don't fuss. I will. Grandma always likes to brush my hair, and anyway, Aunt Samantha doesn't care if I look messy."

"I know," said Mrs. Moffat. "Samantha lets a lot slide, and I think Packer now he's retired looks down the neck of a bottle once too often." (That meant he drank whiskey in the evening. Sally knew that with Prohibition, whiskey was not legal.)

Mrs. Moffat paused to make sure Sally was concentrating on what she was about to say. "I am going to rely on you, Sally, to be sensible, cautious, quick to help, quiet, articulate, and above all polite and independent."

Sally wanted to giggle. It was impossible to be all those things at one time. But she merely nodded solemnly and thought about how she was going to grow up and live with Grandma in the mountains her whole lifetime, and have a dozen cats, a banjo, short-short dresses and short hair, and long pants, and not fuss like her mother.

"Let's get that good alligator suitcase I took to Florida last winter," said Mrs. Moffat.

"I'd rather have my blue camp bag. It's not so heavy."

"The alligator is rich-looking. People notice these things."

"Who? What people?"

"Sally dear, you must try always to look your best—

well, ladylike, and of good background."

"Ma! It's only to Cottersville. Who worries about stuff like that?"

"I do, dear. One has to think of these things."

Lately, it seemed to Sally that conversations tended to go around in silly circles that went nowhere. Decisively, she said, "If I'm going Saturday, let's pack."

14

Chapter III

Sally sat alone in the rear of the Paige. She'd been sit=
ting for two hours, but it felt like two hundred. The
plush seat was hot and itchy. Heat shimmered up from
the pavement ahead. Her father wasn't talking much,
and she was bored with the paper dolls spread around
her. Sally stuck her head out the window to see better.
"Hey, Dad, the dirt's turned pink."

"Yes, we're getting up there."

Of course. The Catskills' bones are pink—that's what
Grandma said. The hills were getting steeper and
steeper. The trees had changed from maples to pines.
There were no longer roadside weeds, only pinkish
pebbles and rocks. Mr. Moffat changed into second gear
at the pitch of the hill. He liked automobiles and didn't
want to be distracted while he drove. Sally stayed quiet

and counted pines and tried for a glimpse of the mountain brook that gurgled below the road. "Pull your head in before you fall out and break your neck," her father yelled over the motor. "Stay put awhile longer, and we'll stop at the Halfway Spring."

Sally propped her sandals on her suitcase. She licked a finger and tried to rub off a smudge on one toe. She worried. The sandals were too new to be scuffed. Then she relaxed. Grandma and Aunt Samantha never fumed, like her mother, over scuffs or scratches.

"Out for a short stop." Her father swung the car off the pavement and parked beside a pile of rocks. Water gushed from a pipe. "I'm going to let the car cool a minute," said Mr. Moffat. He unsnapped two latches at the side of the hood and folded the side over the top. He tapped the temperature gauge mounted on the outside radiator cap. "Hot day."

Sally leaned over the fountain. The water was so icy that it made her teeth ache. She wiped the drips off her chin with her wrists and fanned the drops out of the skirt of her new red-and-blue-flowered cotton dress. Her mother sewed dresses large enough for Sally to grow into. This skirt was too long, especially when the style was for very short ones. It annoyed Sally. She drank again, then her father's voice made her jump. "What the Sam Hill!"

A cloud of dust ballooned around them. A shiny black Buick, too close to the shoulder of the road, sprayed them with dirt and gravel. "Wonder if that fool knows what he's doing. Never make it to the top at that rate," Mr. Moffat said. He brushed at his shirt. "He's still got fourteen hairpin curves to brake and shift on."

Sally stared after the car. A girl, with glasses on her nose and stylish short dark hair, peered out the ellipse of the rear window. The girl smiled and knocked at the glass. "Was that a girl waving out the window?" Sally asked.

Mr. Moffat held his tie out of the water and bent to drink. "Didn't notice. Nice car though. City license plates. Those city drivers don't know how to treat a good automobile . . . don't know what they're doing off Broadway. Hunh!" Mr. Moffat cleared his throat and spat in the ditch. Sally remembered that the last trip they'd had to the city, he'd gotten lost in Central Park, but she decided not to remind him.

Mr. Moffat stared up the mountain. "Jewish, I suppose. More and more of 'em cluttering up the mountains. Get in, chickadee, let's go."

Sally recalled, once they were on the way again, that her father had complained last summer about crowds of vacationers, as if he owned the mountains. He said he couldn't find a place to park on Main Street, or buy a gallon of maple syrup for under a dollar. "Prices driven up on everything." Aunt Samantha had only laughed at him and said that more people meant more business, and that was good for her shop.

17

Aunt Samantha had opened Ye Olde Gifte Shoppe when Uncle Packer had retired from the bank. She said one of them had to keep working so they wouldn't get on each other's nerves around the house. Aunt Samantha said what she meant, no beating around the bush. She was outspoken and also very generous. Sally had gone home with a big haul of odds and ends from the shop last summer.

"There!" Her father pointed through the windshield and sounded quite satisfied. "I didn't think he'd get far."

Pulled to the side of the road was the black Buick. The driver, a large man in full knickers and a brown cap, stood in front of a cloud of steam that was whirling out of the radiator. "Aren't you going to stop?" asked Sally. "Oh!" There was the girl she had seen through the window. She stood beside the man. She had a pert face framed with dark hair and a pink bow on top. Her pink, flounced dress was nifty, very short. Its hem came much farther up her thighs than Sally's mother allowed. As Sally and her father chugged by, the girl pushed her glasses up the bridge of her nose, then waved at Sally again. Someone else stirred in the front seat. Was it the mother? "Is she waving at us to stop?" Sally said.

"Can't help him," said Mr. Moffat. "He'll have to let it cool off by itself." He chuckled. "City cars. City people. They both run hot, you know what I mean." Sally didn't, but she giggled because she knew her father meant her to. She did not think it was nice to drive right by. Her

18

father could have driven them back to Halfway Spring for water. She understood him though. Someone had covered him with dirt and dust; let that someone get what was coming to him. Mr. Moffat had a tough-mindedness that made Sally uncomfortable. She had heard him say to Colin or Sam after a bloody-nosed scrap with another boy, "You have to give as good as you get, fair or foul, kids. *Fair* or *foul*."

They were almost in Cottersville. "Can't this car go any faster?" Sally asked. She wanted to get to the cottage and get *out*.

They came to the beginning stores of Main Street, down one gentle roll of hill and up another. Sally saw Aunt Samantha's shop looking spruce and inviting. With her father muttering, the Paige went on through busy traffic to the outskirts of town, where the big hotels were. They turned left and started up Clemens Hill. Sally's heart beat faster. There was the cottage. Good, Aunt Samantha hadn't repainted it. It was still a spotless white. Sally was out of the car almost before the yellow-spoked wheels had stopped rolling. She ran up the steps to the sunporch. "We're here!" she called through the screen door. She yanked it open and ran between wicker chairs to the kitchen. "Where's everybody? Grandma! We're here."

Grandma came to the doorway between the dining room and kitchen. The late afternoon sun lit up her silvery curls like a halo. It was glorious, that hair. Last

19

summer Aunt Samantha had cut it with her sewing shears because Grandma said that she could no longer get her hands back to plait it up. Grandma was not much taller than Sally. Her skin was brown and wrinkly from the sun. Her name was Sarah-Mariah, to rhyme with briar, and Sally was named after her. Now she held out her ginghamed arms. "There's Sally m'lally," she said. Sally hugged Grandma so hard, she said, "Oof. Young'un, you'll have the breath right out of me." Her voice was gentle but clear as a mountain rill. It never complained or went impatient like Sally's parents'.

"I'm so glad to see you!" Sally said. She was flooded with feelings of affection, and repeated, "Grandma, I am just so *glad* to see you." She caught Grandma's scent, partly freshly ironed clothes, partly a peppery whiff of Grandma's candy, preserved ginger.

"I am mighty pleased to see you too," said Grandma. She put her arm around Sally's waist and shoved her glasses up for a better look. "Taller than I am now. Grown another six inches, I judge. All stalk and no leaf," she said, pinching Sally's ribs. She clacked her false teeth, and Sally laughed.

Uncle Packer, tall and a bit stooped, loomed behind Grandma. He bent and brushed Sally's cheek with his walrus mustache. "Glad you're here, girlie," he said. Just then Mr. Moffat struggled into the kitchen with the heavy alligator suitcase. "Let me help you with that, Perry."

Looking out the window, Sally saw Aunt Samantha, a

poor driver at best, skid into her driveway and jerk to a stop beside the Paige. Everyone could hear the tinny bang as her car came to rest against Mr. Moffat's fender.

"Uh-oh," said Uncle Packer. He opened the door and went out. Sally's father said nothing, but he was down the sun-porch steps in a hurry.

Sally and Grandma, side by side, went outside to see too. "Sam'tha's too fast for her own good," said Grandma.

"Hi, everybody. Sorry I'm late." Aunt Samantha emerged in a bright paisley print dress short enough to show her knees. "I'm a little close to your car," she said unconcernedly.

Then all the grown-ups began talking at once. Sally could not get a word in edgewise and decided to check to make sure every room in the cottage was still the same. You never knew when Aunt Samantha might sell something, or change the furniture around.

She walked through the kitchen into the dining room. She ran her hand over the polished top of the walnut table, peered through the curved glass of the china closet at Aunt Samantha's cut-glass bowls and cake plates.

To her right the living room opened wide before her. Sally liked its conglomeration of furniture, but her mother had said there was no accounting for Aunt Samantha's taste. Aunt Samantha had brought Navajo rugs from when she lived in New Mexico, and set her new cut-velvet sofa and chairs on top of them. There were white walls, to set off the dark wood of the windowsills

31

and baseboard, and Sally liked to see the gleam of waxed floors around the colorful rugs.

Good, they had not gotten rid of the stuffed Arctic owl on top of the cabinet. Sally stopped by his birch log and thrust her fingers into the soft down of his breast. His wings were raised above his head; his eyes were fierce and yellow, and his beak was splendidly hooked and threatening.

The blond piano was there too. It was different from most grands. It was a rectangle, and it was inlaid across the front with ebony and mother-of-pearl. The designs were of scalloped shells, dolphins, and a mermaid, full-breasted and, as Sam had pointed out, "with nipples!" Sally found the piano fascinating. She played several chords, singing to them, "I'm here, here, he-e-e-ere."

She closed the lid. What next? Run upstairs and check the Fort? That's what she and Sam and Colin called their special hiding place, under the eaves off the room they shared. But this summer it would be hers alone. Oh, but she couldn't do everything at once, and she *must* visit the Pine Grove. She had to see if the hammock was still hung between the same trees. Sally dashed out the front door and ran all the way to Aunt Samantha's private pine woods. She breathed deeply of the good balsam-scented mountain air. Suddenly her throat locked, and she began choking. Whoop. Whoop. Gasp, cough, choke, whoop. She'd thought she was cured. Rats. Whoo-ooop. She struggled to get her breath. She had to calm down and stop that awful, chest-heaving choking. She supposed she had run too fast. She walked out of the Pine Grove, but didn't see clearly where she was going. Everything went misty because her eyes were watering like Niagara. She stumbled over a lump of granite hidden beneath grass and fell, *oomph*.

That knocked the rest of the wind out of her. She fell to her knees. Oh dear. Choking like that meant she was going to vomit. Suddenly she felt Grandma's long starched skirts rustling at her side. Sally heaved up her lunch while Grandma leaned over her and smoothed her perspiring forehead. Grandma said, "All right, all right. Rest a moment, dear." Sally sat on the rock. She sniffed with distaste at the nausea and the smell, but her terror at being unable to breathe began to melt away.

While Sally recovered, Grandma went back to the garage and returned with a garden spade. The handle was taller than she was, but she jabbed the spade twice into the earth and covered the puddle Sally had left with pink Catskill dirt and roots. Then she leaned the spade against Sally's rock and sat beside her. "All my children had the whooping cough, one time or another, and there were nine of them." Grandma fumbled in her apron pocket. She took out a small tin and held it out to Sally. Candied Jamaica ginger. Ginger was so much a part of Grandma. "Nibble it," said Grandma. "Settles the stomach." She put a piece in her own mouth.

The taste was hot and burning on Sally's tongue. It was lovely. They sucked together. Sally felt at ease,

23

much better than she'd felt since June. She put her finger through one of Grandma's silvery white curls. "Your hair's gotten even curlier, Grandma."

Grandma made her little "Hmmmp" sound. It was the sound she made when she was amused or interested. "Last time I told Sam'tha to cut it shorter. That made it curl more."

"My hair's grown so long this summer," said Sally. "I don't know that I like braids."

"I fancy it long," said Grandma. She patted one braid between gnarled fingers, then took off her glasses as she did when she wanted to look close. "See better without 'em anymore," she said in her low, crisp voice, "and I imagine you're getting hungry enough for supper. Come wash up."

"Yes. I'm starving. Grandma, did you bake a squash pie with ginger in it?"

Grandma's smile creased up her brown cheeks and added more wrinkles on top of the ones that never went away. "What makes you think I would do that?"

"Two things we always have when I come, Grandma, squash pies and a picnic at Stone Bridge at least once. Are we going to this year?"

Grandma lifted Sally's hand and brushed it along her petal-soft cheek. "Of course," she said.

"That's just . . . perfect," said Sally. "Like you. Perfect."

"Nonsense." Grandma was matter-of-fact. "Nobody's

perfect. Certainly not your old grandma."

"Sure you are, Grandma," said Sally, "and your squash-and-ginger pies're the perfectest of all."

Grandma pushed herself up by leaning on the spade. "That's not good grammar," she said. She started across the drive using the spade like a large cane. "Grandchild, there's no such thing as perfect. Best pie I ever made was a mistake. I used up the end of a can of cloves I thought was ginger. Mistake made it extra good. Sometimes it's the flaw that comes through best." She nodded at Sally. "Sometimes it's the stroke of genius. Flaws make the world go round."

"Grandma, I really, really just *love* you," Sally said.

25

CHAPTER IV

The first thing that Sally saw when she opened her eyes in the morning was the triangular ceiling of her room. She blinked into the bright blue of the window under the eaves and remembered she was at the cottage. Joy! The pine boards chilled her bare toes, but she leaped to the seat in the dormer window and knelt to look out, shivering. An orange cat sashayed past on Clemens Hill Road. His tail jutted perfectly straight in the air. No, Grandma had said there was no such thing as perfection. Sure enough, when Sally looked more closely, she saw that at the last inch, the tail curved into a question mark. Sally laughed out loud. As if he knew he was being watched, the cat dove into the high grass and disappeared.

Sally unlatched a small door into the storage attic

under the eaves that made the area Sally and her brothers called the Fort. She turned on the light and crouched to enter. Two stools and an old chair stood on the piece of carpet Aunt Samantha had given them. A bookcase, one leg propped on a coffee can, held books and other treasures. There was her elephant bead bracelet. Sally blew the dust off and put it on. The tiny white elephants held each other's tails and marched about her wrist. It was a gift-shop cast-off, and she'd thought she had lost it.

"Break-fa-a-a-ast." Aunt Samantha's voice carried up the stairway. "If you want to go to the shop with me, hurry for cor-r-rn ca-akes."

"I'm coming." For as long as Sally could remember, she had spent the first day of her mountain vacations with Aunt Samantha exploring Ye Shoppe. She splashed water on her face, stuck her tongue out at the toothbrush, pulled on her favorite green slacks and a blue-and-green shirt, and grabbed a sweater. Grandma would help with her braids after breakfast.

In the kitchen, the oven door was open and the gas was on. Looking smaller than usual, Grandma sat near the stove hunched into her lavender shawl. She dipped a piece of dry toast into a cup of hot water. "Morning, Sally," she said. Her voice was a little hoarse.

Aunt Samantha wore a large apron more or less covering her smart silk dress. She poured batter on a griddle. "Just in time. I'll go prod Packer again." She disap-

27

peared down the hall.

There was a smell of scorching. "I think the corn cakes are burning," said Sally. She took the spatula and turned them. The edges were scarred black.

Aunt Samantha returned. "What a slugabed Packer is. Never mind a little burn, Sally. Use more syrup." Food did not interest Aunt Samantha. She liked household gadgets, sewing machines, vacuum cleaners, paint sprayers. She had a doughnut machine that turned out queer, three-sided doughnuts. Sally ate the charred corn cakes but refused seconds.

Grandma sucked at a crust and eyed Aunt Samantha. "Never fatten the child that way," she said. "*I* get dinner and supper. I'd get the breakfast too, but it's so cold now, mornings." Grandma drew her shawl tighter and glared into her cup. Steam rose and fogged her glasses. "Shah!" she said as if the weather were held in her cup.

They finished breakfast. Aunt Samantha went out to the car, but was back before Grandma had braided Sally's hair.

"What a blamed nuisance," she said. "Car won't start."

"It's like me these cold mornings," said Grandma. "Hmmmp-hmmmp."

"I knew, when we built this house on a hill, it was good for starting cars," Aunt Samantha said. "Tell your uncle to come out and give us a shove over the crest."

Sally had to get Uncle Packer out of bed. He grunted and groaned and put on a blue flannel bathrobe. "Told her Ed ought to look at that battery," he said as he followed Sally out to the car.

Aunt Samantha sat up high behind the steering wheel. She rolled down the window. "Get in, Sally, dear, so Packer can get us started." She motioned out the window for Packer to start pushing. A short distance down the hill, the motor turned over and began to roar. "There," said Aunt Samantha and shifted into third gear. They gathered speed, but when they had to stop behind a horse and wagon, the motor died. They were only at the bottom of Clemens Hill and had come less than a mile. Grossman's Mountain House Hotel stretched out to their right; a cottage in a flower garden was across the street.

"Shall I go up for Uncle Packer?"

"No point now," said Aunt Samantha. "We've run out of hill." She got out of the car. "I'll have to crank the machine.

Sally climbed down too and realized they were in full view of a bunch of children on the hotel's porch. She looked with interest at Grossman's collection of white-and-green-painted buildings, connected by long porches. The paint was fresh, the green rocking chairs new. She didn't think it had looked so spiffy last year. She glanced again at the children. They were grinning. It was Aunt Samantha, of course. In her good dress and high-heeled pumps, she looked strange to be a car mechanic. Aunt Samantha did not worry about such things. Spraddling her legs wide and bending double, she inserted the crank at the bottom of the radiator. She pumped the handle around to start the motor. The car only sputtered. The children left the porch and moved to the sidewalk. "She's got it," said one boy in a sailor suit.

"No, she hasn't."

"Bet she can't do it either."

"It's awful hard to crank a car."

Sally blinked with recognition. One of the children was the dark-haired girl from the car Mr. Moffat had passed on the highway. The girl recognized Sally at the same time. "Hello," she said. "Do you want my father to help you?" She beckoned at a line of rocking chairs on the porch. A tall man in white flannels rose. He took a cigar from his mouth and walked down the steps. On the last one, he balanced the cigar.

"Allow me to do it, please," he said to Aunt Samantha. He had a deep voice with a hint of an accent.

"Most kind of you," said Aunt Samantha. Her cloche hat had fallen over one eye. She righted it and stepped aside.

The girl kept smiling at Sally as if she were a dear friend. "My name's Evie," she said. "What's yours?"

"Sally." At once Sally was aware of how faded her slacks were. Evie wore beautiful crimson shorts. She had a fuzzy angora sweater over a pink blouse and a red bow in her hair. Her smile was very warm. Feeling dowdy, Sally also remembered that her father had not stopped to help yesterday, and that he had sneered about Jews. If this girl was staying at this hotel, she'd *be* Jewish, wouldn't she? Sally frowned in anxiety.

"Don't worry," said Evie. "My father can make it work. He's very strong. Is that your mother?"

"That's my Aunt Samantha," said Sally. "I'm staying with her for a few weeks."

"My father is Morton Grauber," said Evie. She said the name as if it were important, as if Sally ought to know it. Sally said nothing.

"Where are you going with your aunt?" Evie stood close to Sally. She was shorter and plumper. Grandma would have liked how well-rounded she was. "I wish I was going someplace. This hotel is full of *little* kids. Are you going somewhere I can go with you when you go?"

"Uh. Well. Only downtown." In spite of her long summer at home without friends Sally did not feel welcoming. She had counted on Aunt Samantha's undivided attention and the chance to hunt through the shop by herself. Sally said, "Uh, I'm getting over whooping cough. I've had it all summer." Probably Evie would not want to go now, not if she might catch something horrid like that. Sally hoped.

But: "That's okay. I already had it when I was young," she said. The car finally roared to life. Evie's father stood up and gave the crank to Aunt Samantha. His face was the color of a cooked beet. Evie giggled. "See, my father puts a lot of effort into everything he does."

"Thank you so very much," said Aunt Samantha. "I could never have done that myself. Ready, Sally?"

"Wait, wait!" Evie sounded anxious. "Daddy, this is

31

Sally and her Aunt Samantha, and she wants me to go with her for a little while. That's swell, isn't it, and I can go, can't I?" Sally was appalled. She had not really invited this girl. Sally wanted Aunt Samantha to say there was no room or no time, or at least tell the girl no, not today. But Aunt Samantha was conferring with Mr. Grauber, and Sally could not hear them over the racing motor.

Then Evie climbed into the car, pushing Sally over so there would be room for three on the front seat. She acted as if she had known Sally and Aunt Samantha her whole life. "Isn't this fun?" The girl's chin was level with Sally's shoulder. She dug it into Sally's collarbone and pinched her arm. "I'm so glad I get to go with you," she said.

What was happening? Aunt Samantha was nodding and smiling and shaking hands with Mr. Grauber. They were going, and taking Evie with them!

Evie waved happily at her father and the other children. They turned the corner into Main Street and headed for the busier part of the village. Stores were open, but the streets were fairly empty. They'd be bursting by midmorning.

"All right, girls," said Aunt Samantha, once they had stopped in front of the shop. "Invite your friend in, Sally, and let's see what's in the morning mail."

My *friend*? thought Sally. She liked to choose her own friends, not have them drop on her out of the blue like that. Annoyed, she waited on the sidewalk with Evie,

32

while Aunt Samantha searched through her purse for the key.

Sally glanced down Cottersville's hilly Main Street. The Hasbrouck's Jewelry sign glittered with gilt. The mountains beyond the town showed blue in the far sunshine and set off the wooden and brick buildings that lined both sides of the street. There was new paint on Zweifel's, the plumber's, and a crack in the glass of the barber's pole.

Evie said in Sally's ear, "I love sidewalks on hills, don't you? I love roller-skating, don't you?"

Though she had ball-bearing, steel-wheeled skates she was proud of at home, Sally felt like being grumpy. "There are lots of other things to do in the mountains," she said. Aunt Samantha unlocked the door. Sally followed her but rudely pulled at the door to close it behind her. Evie had to hurry through, and slipped in so close she trod Sally's foot out of her sneaker at the heel. "Watch what you're doing," said Sally.

"Oooo, I'm sorry. Did that hurt?" Evie's gray eyes, magnified behind her glasses, looked worriedly at Sally out of all proportion to the injury.

"Forget it," said Sally. She hated being so sour, but she could not stop herself. Evie did not worry long. She hastened down one aisle and up another and picked up objects to admire.

"I'd like this," she said, "and this, and this, and this here." She chose an enameled pin box, a small brass door knocker, a striped tiger of spun glass. She shook a hol-

33

low paperweight that snowed a miniature blizzard, and wound up a Swiss music box that tinkled "The Waltz of the Flowers." "You're awful lucky to have so much to choose from."

"It isn't mine," said Sally. "It's Aunt Samantha's. Be careful or you'll break something."

Aunt Samantha was going through a flat basket of mail. "Sally, will you go to the butcher's for me, before he gets busy? Grandma wants a pot roast, and sausage. Here, take her list. You can get the rest at Osterhoudt's while you're shopping." Osterhoudt was the greengrocer.

Sally really wanted to hunt around the shop, but with Evie there, so brash and nosy, she was willing to put off the pleasure.

"Sure," Sally said. "Do I charge it or pay?"

"Ask to have it put on my bill," said Aunt Samantha.

Evie stuck her arm through Sally's, which was silly, because they bumped and got stuck going double through the door. "You first," said Sally. She did not want her heel scraped again.

Evie had felt the elephant bracelet under Sally's sleeve. She pulled up the sweater to see. "Oooo, how cute." She pushed a finger under the bracelet and turned it around Sally's wrist. "Can I have it?" Sally could hardly believe her ears. "*You* know," said Evie, "let me wear it one day, and I'll let you wear something of mine, okay?" Sally shook her head. She was sure Evie had nothing that she wanted.

34

They stopped in front of Carter's Bakery. The ovens must have been just opened. Evie breathed in and out noisily. "Unnnn, ahhhh. Chocolate. I love chocolate, don't you?"

Inhaling the scent of fresh cakes, Sally had to agree. Her mouth watered at the smell, but she snapped, "Hurry up. Here's the butcher's." The next window was embossed with white letters, VANDERDONCK'S FINE MEATS. The door was open, and they scuffed in through the sawdust that covered the floor.

"Can you wait on us?" Sally asked the butcher. "I have a list for Mrs. Mead."

He put his hands on the counter on either side of the list and smiled at them both. "Certainly. I'll get them especially good. Let's see, which of the old lady's grandchildren are you?"

"Sally Moffat."

"And your cousin?" said Mr. Vanderdonck. He looked at Evie, who tittered.

"No, she's not my cousin. She's staying at Grossman's."

Mr. Vanderdonck put a cylinder of baloney on the chopping block and shaved off two slices with his enormous cleaver. He extended his hands over the counter, holding a slice in each. "Please?" he said.

Sally took hers gratefully. Mr. Vanderdonck's baloney was better than anybody's, and he cut thick slices. Evie took hers, but whispered to Sally, "I bet it's pork."

"So what?" said Sally.

Evie said, "I'm not supposed to eat it."

35

Sally was mystified. She did not want Evie to turn down the gift and hurt Mr. Vanderdonck's feelings. "I'll eat it if you don't want it. Why aren't you supposed to?"

Evie giggled.

"They don't want you to eat between meals?"

Evie tried a small bite. The bites became larger and larger till only the rind was left. Evie tried to feed it to the butcher's cat. Sally thought that she acted sort of dumb.

Mr. Vanderdonck wrapped the order in separate packages so they could take turns carrying the heavier items. At the greengrocer's, they stopped to buy the fruits and vegetables from Grandma's list, then returned to the gift shop. Sally placed the packages in the rear to stay cool. Evie made no move to go home, and after all, she could have walked if she had wanted to. Sally sighed. Well, she'd have to begin the serious business of checking the glass cases and racks of souvenirs with Evie looking on. Sally liked to dream about the contents of the cases—imagine herself wearing a particular necklace, for instance.

This time Evie did not pause to look at the stock at all. There were two or three customers in the shop, and she walked up to one of the women. "Maybe I can help you?" Evie said. Sally expected the woman to laugh.

But the woman, who was stroking first one scarf and then another, said, "Which would *you* buy for a girl about your age? Which do you like?"

Evie was grave. "It depends. Is she blond like Sally,

there, or dark like me? You want a color to complement the skin tones, don't you?" Skin tones! What kind of guff was that?

Evie dug into the pile, pulled out scarves, and unfolded them. She held one up to the light. "Now, take this," Evie said. "Feel how soft." She held a rose-and-white plaid scarf to the woman's cheek. "See in the mirror, now nice it goes? You like it, the little girl will like it."

The woman actually bought the scarf Evie had picked out and left smiling. "Come again," Evie called after her.

Pleased as punch, Evie glanced around for Sally's approval. She explained, "Sometimes, you got to make up the customer's mind for her. Indecision, it hurts them."

"How do you know about customers?" said Sally. She herself had never thought to wait on anybody.

Evie shrugged. "Easy. I help my mother once in a while. When *she* helps out in busy seasons, that is. My father owns a real big store, not bitsy like this. It's fun. Come on, you try."

"I don't know what to say."

"Can I help you, that's all, dopey." Evie gave Sally a nudge.

"It's *may*," said Sally. "*May* I help you?"

"Why yes, you may," a man said behind her. Sally whirled around. He grinned at her. "Do you have playing cards with views of the Catskills?" She was stuck with it, willy-nilly. She brought out boxes of cards, offered souvenir pencils, painted bells, and postcards. By noontime, she had a cobweb on one braid from climbing into the storeroom for leftover lanterns, and her stomach growled with hunger. She had not coughed once, and she never had a chance to dream over the shelves. Neither had she ever felt so wide-awake and useful before. "Golly," Sally said. "We must have made a load of money!"

"Peanuts, this stuff," said Evie. "My father sells furs. You should see the prices. But it was fun, wasn't it?"

"I have to reward such devoted helpers," said Aunt Samantha. "Pick out one of these barrettes." She opened a velvet case of enameled hair barrettes. Evie almost snatched a red-flowered one and held it to her hair. Sally took longer to decide. When she settled on blue flowers, Evie changed her mind.

"Trade with me? You get the red, and give me the blue?"

Sally was irritated. "You had first choice. You wanted the red one."

"I think I like the blue better." Silently, Sally handed over the blue barrette. Evie giggled and poked Sally. What was so funny? Sally seethed but said nothing.

When Aunt Samantha's helper arrived, the three of them left the shop. The car started without a hitch. They drove out on Main Street and turned left at Clemens Hill.

Aunt Samantha dropped Evie off in front of Grossman's Hotel. "I'll be up to see you soon," Evie promised. "Thank you for a very nice time."

"There now," said Aunt Samantha as they pulled away. "You have a new friend to help occupy your time."

"Uh, well," said Sally. Her foot rustled against paper. Sally picked up a tissue packet. It was the blue barrette. Evie must have dropped it on the floor.

"You can give it to her when you see her again," said Aunt Samantha.

"I'm not sure she really wanted it," said Sally. "She said her father owns a much bigger store." Sally had an inkling that Evie had been making fun of Ye Olde Gifte Shoppe . . . "peanuts" was what Evie had said of the prices, and "bitsy" store.

Sally decided she wanted to put out of her mind that Evie, with her expensive clothes and titters over baloney in the meat market. She did not need any other reminder either of the big car that had scattered dust on her father. Trying to sound adult to Aunt Samantha, Sally said, "On the whole, I do not believe I care for that girl very much." She tucked the rejected barrette in her pocket. She was almost certain Evie had dropped it on purpose. "She's only a summer visitor."

CHAPTER V

On Wednesday, Sally washed several pairs of socks and underpants and pinned them to the clothesline outside. It was a good drying day, Grandma had said at breakfast.

Aunt Samantha was still home. When Sally went inside, she was standing at the head of the cellar stairs. "Mother," she called, "are you down there?"

Sally heard the clinking of crockery and bottles being moved, then Grandma's voice, "Sam'tha, I can't find those huckleberry pails."

Aunt Samantha snorted in disgust. She said to Sally, "I've told her and told her not to go down those cellar steps. They're too steep. She's going to fall and break a hip, and that will be a fine howdy-do." She raised her voice. "Mother, come *up* here. I threw those old pails

40

away. They were rusty."

"Shah, Sam'tha," said Grandma. She climbed the narrow passage. "*I* know what you're thinkin': what to do with me when I break a leg. Hmmmp-hmmmp."

Aunt Samantha put her hands on her hips. "You know those stairs are easier to come up than they are to go down. They're dark and narrow."

"Fiddledeedee." Grandma was impatient. "Tell me, what will Sally and I pick huckleberries into, a dumpling dish or a pan for a fish?"

Sally was delighted. Grandma was feeling good today, full of jokes and sayings. "*Are* we going to pick huckleberries?"

"We are, surely. It's the huckleberry part of summer. That is, if Sam'tha can spare a receptacle or two," said Grandma. She shook cellar dust out of her skirt.

"I have some nice light baskets from the shop." Aunt Samantha smiled at Sally. "Better take off those shorts and cover your legs. Bound to be briars in a huckleberry meadow."

Sally raced up to her room to change. She put on slacks and a long-sleeved shirt. There might be poison ivy too.

They started out, each with a basket. Sally carried a bag of lunch Grandma had already packed, and Grandma had the lemonade thermos. "A nibble is all we need," she said, blue eyes twinkling at Sally, "to keep our spirits up and our fingers nimble, hm?"

There were few briars, but there was quite a lot of dew in the deep grass. Soon Sally's feet and the bottoms of her slacks were wet. "No matter," said Grandma. "Sun'll dry us in no time." Her own long skirt was dark with dew at the hem. "Guess if I were real modern, I'd wear these short dresses to go with my short hair."

Sally squinted at Grandma's full skirt. "Or pants?" she asked.

"Hmmmp-hmmmp," went Grandma. "Now, grandchild, would you know your old grandma in trousers? 'Sides, when I was growing up, the sheriff might've put me in jail for wearing men's clothes. How times've changed." A grasshopper leaped onto Grandma's skirt. She picked him off between thumb and finger. "Spit t'bacco, hopper," she said. She opened her fingers, and the grasshopper flew away with a whirring clatter. In her hand was a small brown drop.

"It's not tobacco," said Sally, "but what is it?"

"His juices, I expect," said Grandma. "I must have asked hoppers to spit t'bacco for eighty years, and they always do. The men used to chew t'bacco, and spit brown, and that's how we got to say it to the hoppers. I've seen a lot of changes, and some of 'em I like—like no more chewing t'bacco. Nasty habit." Grandma and Sally were walking side by side across an uncultivated field. In some far-off day it had been plowed. The ridges of the old furrows made for bumpy walking. There were a few birch saplings showing white branches here and there and clumps of reddened sumac in the long grass.

"What are the changes you don't like?" said Sally. She paused at a stone wall and watched Grandma set down the thermos and gather her skirt together to step over neatly. Sally hoped she could prod Grandma into talking about the old days. She never tired of hearing how Grandma had walked to her one-room school carrying her shoes and stockings and not put them on until she sat on the school porch. Or how Grandma went sledding in the winter by sliding downhill on barrel staves because she could not afford a sled. Especially, Sally enjoyed hearing Grandma talk about her many children, how Sally's great-uncles and great-aunts had been born in the four-poster that Grandma now slept in, and how great-aunt Samantha had been the last baby and so was nearly Sally's father's age. Sally felt firmly tied to Grandma by all the knots of relationships. "What are the things you don't like about today?" she repeated.

Grandma looked at Sally from under the brim of her old straw hat. It was tied with faded grosgrain under her chin. She point east, away from the mountain they called the Slide, and said, "Tell you what I don't 'preciate atall—those golfing places—fairways? They're abusing some of my best huckleberry patches. Look at that."

Sally looked. In front of them was another uncultivated field, full of huckleberry clumps, but across the barbed wire fence to their right flowed the smooth green undulations of a golf course. Trees grew here and there, and a small pond glistened next to a sandy hollow. The total effect was like a painted picture, a perfection of a landscape with no room for berries.

"Oh!" cried Sally. "That wasn't there last year!"

"Certainly wasn't. Brand-new this spring. Some of the best bushes got rooted up and plowed under." She turned her back on the fairway. "Find some shade to put the lunch in, and let's get to work. I want to make a pie for supper."

"And I can help," said Sally. "I love rolling dough."

"I'm counting on you to make tart shells," said Grandma. They began to collect ripe berries. Each one fell noiselessly from hand to basket. "There now," said Grandma. "I miss those pails. I liked the way the first berries went *plinketty-plunk*. Sam'tha and her new-fangled notions."

"Did you pick huckleberries when you were little?"

A bee buzzed around a huckleberry blossom. Grandma said, "A ton of berries in my time. Huckle-berries, blackberries, raspberries, strawberries. Wild ones, better than the grown stuff Jim Osterhoudt sells. The wild ones are more flavorsome." Stooping by the berry bushes, Grandma looked like a forest gnome to Sally. The back of her sun hat stuck up almost perpen-dicular to her hunched shoulders. Suddenly, *whack* . . . *thud*. Sally ducked at the noise and saw a small white object hit Grandma's hat. The hat flew up and flopped forward over Grandma's face. "What in tarnation was *that*?" Grandma grabbed at her brim.

Sally dug into the curly grass and pulled out a golf

44

ball. "Somebody hit a golf ball way over here. Isn't that funny?"

"No, not so. Not funny," said Grandma. She pursed her lips and sucked in her cheeks. "Downright careless. Might have had my scalp." She retied the ribbon to hold the hat firm. "Some fool out there don't care about other folks' safety, only his own pleasure. I don't know what the world's coming to. No responsibility left for the other fella atall."

"Halloooo." There was a shout from the fairway. A person paused on the other side of the barbed wire, silhouetted against the sky. Sally saw he wore modern wide golf knickers called plus fours. He began to walk closer to the fence at the edge of their huckleberry field.

Sally shaded her eyes. "There's a man hollering. It must be his ball."

Grandma gave one glance and returned to berrying. She moved to a fuller bush.

"Little girl," shouted the man, waving both arms. "Did a ball come over that way?" He stopped at the barbed wire. Probably wouldn't want to climb over, Sally guessed. Now that he was close enough, she could see he was large and tall and looked like Evie's father.

"I think that's Evie's father, Grandma. You know, that girl, Evie, I told you about, who came to the shop with us?" Sally stood up with the ball in her hand.

Grandma went, "Hmmmp-hmmmp." So she was

amused now, and not mad. "I think we ladies might let him come get his ball. Then he can tell us how sorry he is. If you just take that ball over *to* him, he'll say a thank-you-very-much, and that will be it. Let's make him tackle that barbed wire. I want to see him get those big trousers through. Make him come see *me*."

"Well," said Sally. She felt deceitful, standing there with the ball in her hand while an adult asked for it.

"Is he trying to climb through the wire yet?" Grandma asked.

"Yes," said Sally.

"Got stuck, has he?" said Grandma.

"Yes. His knickers are so floppy wide. He's stuck on the top wire, oh, and on the bottom too. He's trying to pull the barbs away from his knees."

"He'll think twice where he hits his golf ball 'thout looking," said Grandma. "These city people think they own the earth, when it's the other way around."

Sally remembered her father's comment about city people. She said, "Daddy said the Jews are taking over the mountains."

Grandma clacked her teeth. She had not liked that statement. "Perry is surely narrow-minded," said Grandma.

"But you said these city people . . ." began Sally.

Grandma was sharp. "I don't like careless people knocking my hat off. But I'm not a labeler. You know what I mean by a labeler? Call people Baptists and mean one whole set of facts. Call people Jews and mean another whole set of facts. Never true."

"Well," said Sally, trying to sort things out, "that man didn't rip up the bushes himself, so you can't be mad at him for that, but oh, Grandma! 'City people' is a label, isn't it?"

Grandma pulled down her glasses and looked at Sally over the rims. "Ye-es. You'll do, grandchild. Grow up thinking for yourself, that's my Sally m'lally. Just the same, I'm teaching that *city* person a lesson, because I'm old and mean and know better. Hmmmp-hmmmp. Has that city person got his pants clear? Is he coming this way yet?"

"He's walking through the bushes."

Grandma stood erect and steadied her full basket on a rock. "Let me have that thing." She took the ball from Sally. "Now we can be neighborly and meet him halfway 'cause he's on our side of the fence." Grandma had her own rules of fair play.

Evie's father politely took off his linen cap when he saw Grandma and Sally approaching. He was perspiring from his battle with the fence. Sally noticed he had a tear in his knickers. His first words were, "I am very sorry my ball fell over there. I hope it was not near you, madam."

Grandma held up the ball. She only came up to the middle button of Mr. Grauber's shirt, but her stance was regal. "Now sir," she said, "that ball struck my hat *spang* on the brim. Pretty near thing. Might've struck me or the child here. Been hurtful if it had."

47

Evie's father put his cap and golf club under his left arm and clutched his belt buckle. It was a large silver one with a fancy G on it. "Madam, I would not hurt you or a child ever," he said. "You have my deepest apologies. Tell me what I can do, to, to . . ." He struggled for the correct phrase.

"To make amends?" said Grandma. Even stirred up and angry, Grandma was ready to help anybody.

"Yes, yes," said Mr. Grauber. He put his hand in his pocket. "May I give you, ah, uh, the little girl, who I think is a friend of my daughter's, a dollar for something nice?" He smiled at Sally. She decided he really was a nice man. A whole dollar for herself!

"Certainly not!" snapped Grandma. Mr. Grauber took his hand out of his pocket as if it had a hot coal in it.

"Here's your ball, young man. I know you intended no harm. Though you didn't think to look much beyond your own intentions, knocking that little object into a hole, I expect. When you play games—hm?—open your eyes to whatever else is there besides you. There's more here than space for golf balls. Real live folks live in these mountains and have for a hundred and fifty years. We're used to living and let living." Grandma sure was riled. She produced a handkerchief from her sleeve and wiped around her mouth. Her hand trembled a little.

"Yes, madam," said Evie's father. At first he scowled, but then he cleared his throat and smiled. "Thank you for letting me use your mountains." His eyes crinkled up for a moment, and he resembled Evie helping a cus-

48

tomer. "I promise I will learn to look around me. Shall we shake hands on it?" He shook Grandma's knotty-knuckled hand, then Sally's stained with huckleberry juice. Then he bowed slightly and tramped back toward the fence and the fairway.

"Do you think he has an accent, sort of foreign?" asked Sally.

Grandma was indifferent. She had made her point and that was enough. "I don't know." She sighed. "Let's go get the lunch. Too much confabulation. It's made me hungry."

They walked back to where they had been picking berries and took the lunch and the thermos into the shade of some pines. It was cool and soft on the fallen needles after the hot field. "Sometimes I find a little wintergreen in here," said Grandma. "Even in the summer. Makes a nice change from ginger."

Sally began to salivate as soon as Grandma unpacked rolls of waxed paper that were twisted tight at each end. "Try one of these deviled eggs," said Grandma. "I put the mustard in myself. Sam'tha always forgets."

They finished the eggs with bread and wedges of cheese, celery, and the lemonade. Grandma brushed away crumbs. "I figure we'll have dessert after we make pies," she said. "Best get back to picking so we have full baskets for all I plan to make this afternoon."

They returned to the bushes and picked silently. Sally knew Grandma meant business, and it was no time to tease for stories. She picked and perspired, and ate quite

49

a few berries, but even so, her basket got heavier and heavier. At three, Grandma took off her hat and fanned her face. "Got all we can manage, I judge," she said. "We'll go home for a cold drink, shall we? And then start right in on the dough."

Sally stood beside Grandma at the kitchen table. It was well floured so the lump of dough would not stick. Sally pressed down on it with both hands. "Work it thinner," said Grandma. The front doorbell rang, a long and insistent ring. "Let Packer get it. He's snoozing in the living room." She sprinkled more flour on the table. "Now work some more into the dough." Sally folded the lump over and over. Her hands were white to the wrists. "Enough," said Grandma. "Don't make it tough, handling it overmuch. Good crust is tender. Let me see how that feels." She rolled a bit between her palms.

"There's a girl to see Sally," said Uncle Packer. He stood in the arch between the dining room and kitchen. He yawned, and his mustache quivered. "Shall I tell her to come join the baking crew?"

"I better go see," said Sally. There was only one girl it could be . . . Evie. And Sally did not want her disturbing the pie activity. She went out the back hall toward the front door. Sure enough, on the other side of the glass was Evie Grauber with a rainbow-colored jump rope. She swung it at Sally as if to invite her outside to play. Sally did not open the door. "I can't," she shouted and showed her floury hands at the glass. "We're making huckleberry pies." She turned on her heels and returned to the kitchen.

Grandma was stirring cornstarch into a cup of sugar. "Cornstarch sops up the juice inside the crust." Grandma was better than a cookbook.

Knock-knock-knock. "Come in, come in," Uncle Packer yelled.

"Hello," Sally heard Evie say. "Can I talk to Sally, please?" Uncle Packer rattled his newspaper. She guessed he had pointed Evie in the direction of the kitchen, and she was vexed. She thought, Why doesn't Uncle Packer ask *me*?

Evie hopped up the one step. She wore a polka-dot hair bow this time, and her orangy-red dress made her look kind of like a robin with glasses. "I *love* cooking," Evie said. "I'm glad I can come help. I can, can't I?" Sally made her face as negative as possible.

"Come in, dear," Grandma said. She put the berries Sally had sorted and washed into the crust and poured on sugar and cornstarch. "Sally's friends are welcome."

Sally was curt. "This is Evie Grauber. It was her father you talked to this morning, remember?" Sally stood close to Grandma. She did not want to share Grandma or pie making with Evie. She ought to warn her against this stranger. "Evie lives at that Grossman's Hotel."

Grandma smiled. "I'm Mrs. Byrd, Sally's great-grandmother." She pointed to a stool. "Bring that up if you'd like to sit and watch."

51

Evie pulled the stool into place between Sally and Grandma. Sally had to back up or bend forward to see around her. "You're in the way," Sally said. She reached across the table for the flour sifter and shook it so violently that she dusted Evie's lap and bare knees as well as the next lump of dough.

Evie brushed her dress front but only smeared flour deeper into the red. "I better stand like you," Evie said.

"Over here, on my side of the table, is best," said Grandma. "Sally, get some more short'ning from the pantry. Evie can help make tart shells."

Whump. Swish. Sally hit the swinging door into the pantry hard and returned with the can of Crisco. She banged the tin on the table so heavily that the colander of huckleberries jiggled. "I'll just take that, thank you," said Grandma after a bit of teeth clacking. "Sally, do you remember the 'portions for piecrust? You can show Evie." Sally began to shake her head. She did not want to show Evie how to do anything.

"When I was your age," said Grandma, "or maybe a wee bit older, I used to do pies and dumplings and cakes. Had to. My ma had so many children younger'n me. The summer I was twelve, yes, I believe so, that was the summer my brother Franklin was born. . . . I did the cooking for the mowers that year." She handed the mixing spoon and the big tan bowl with the white stripes around it to Sally. "Take a lump of short'ning as big as a walnut, remember?" she said.

Sally measured flour and Crisco and salt. Evie leaned in close to see.

"At first, I thought I couldn't do it . . . cook for those great-bodied men," said Grandma. "But Ma said I could, and she was right." Her gentle voice went on and on as if she were urging Sally, with her hand on Sally's hand, to be generous with Evie. Slowly Sally began to feel soothed, and professional even, like a chef.

"It's important not to overwork the dough," Sally said to Evie as she mixed.

"I think we have enough for another pie before we make tarts," said Grandma, "so Evie can have a chance to roll it, too, hm?"

Sally separated the dough in the bowl and put a lump on the floured table. Evie rolled and rolled while Sally watched her with the eye of an eagle. When the circle was large enough, Grandma said, "I'll just put that in the tin for you. That's very nice, dear." She lowered the crust into the pie tin. Evie pushed in close again to see.

"Don't jostle," said Sally. "You'll make her tear it."

Grandma pressed the dough into the sides of the tin. "Gently does best," she said. She smiled calmly at Sally. "Sally can roll out the top crust, and Evie can pinch it and patte'n it."

"But Grandma—" Sally loved to pattern the top crust with knife-point designs, but she could not whine at Grandma. She bit her tongue and felt queer. When Evie started to prick out a star on the top crust, Sally could no longer keep silent. "You're making that star lopsided!"

Evie stepped off to get a better view. "Is that bad, Mrs. Byrd?"

"Tastes just as good lopsided."

"That crust isn't pinched together tight either," said Sally. Evie fumbled at the edges. She dropped her knife on the floor. When she leaned to retrieve it, she hit the table with her head and knocked a half cup of sugar to the linoleum. Evie kneeled to scrape up sugar with her hands. "You haven't finished the star yet," Sally observed.

"It's all right," said Grandma. "Enough to let the steam out is all." She took the pie and popped it into the oven. "My goodness, nothing would ever get done if a body'd wait till he could do it so perfect no one could find fault with it. Get the whisk broom for Evie. Now we'll *all* do the tarts."

They made twenty-four small huckleberry tarts, as well as the two pies. Without being asked, Evie helped Grandma scrape the dough off the table and put the mixing bowl in the sink to soak in cold water. Sally was still uncomfortable. She needed to get rid of her hot, evil feelings and did not know how.

Grandma washed her hands with yellow soap. "Girls, we've worked hard. I think we deserve a pot of tea."

"Mrs. Byrd," said Evie, "can I take home some tarts to my mother and father?"

"Should think so," said Grandma.

Sally exploded. "Grandma!" She, Sally, had picked

54

half of those berries, well, almost half, and in the hot sun. It did not seem fair to give any tarts to Evie, just because she had rolled out a little dough. It was Evie's father who had practically knocked Grandma over with his golf ball. So why should Grandma send beautiful tarts to him by way of this intrusive *person*? This summer visitor. It was not right. Sally knew it was mean-spirited of her to think that, but she did not care. Pettishly, she kicked the stool into its corner.

Grandma glanced at her. She said, "I always like to share what I've worked on." She stooped to open the oven door. A piecrusty, fruity odor filled the kitchen. "Browning nicely," said Grandma. She closed the door and adjusted the gas flame. "Yes, I like to share my vittles. It makes what I eat taste sweeter to me." Grandma looked hard at Sally. Her blue eyes were so steely that Sally felt they could bore a hole right through to her most secret thoughts. "And I never hold a grudge past a mealtime," she added. "Let's have a speck of ginger with our tea."

CHAPTER VI

Sally replaced the box kite on the top shelf of the Fort's bookcase. She had dusted underneath it. She lined up the stools and the chair. They were too stiff that way, and she rearranged them in a circle. No, that was not much better. The truth was that the Fort needed people in order to come to life. Sally, feeling lonesome, crawled out of the attic door. It was time to go downstairs and talk to Grandma.

"Grandma," said Sally, "what shall I do today?" Her grandmother sat in a wicker chair on the sun porch. She wore a blue dress figured with black and white leaves. She had her glasses off and was bathing her eyes from a pan of hot water.

"Mmm," said Grandma. She pressed a hot towel over her eyes. "Mmm, need something to do, do you?" The veins stood out blue on the skin of her hands.

Sally sat on a flowered hassock. "Do your eyes hurt?" She laid a hand on her grandmother's knee. She felt how small and bony it was through the starchy fabric of Grandma's long dress.

"No, just old and tired," said Grandma without self-pity. "Sam'tha and Packer went downtown in the car. You're older this summer. Want to walk to town by yourself?" Sally knew immediately that going for a walk and exploring by herself was what she needed. "Time to flutter your wings," said Grandma. She removed the towel. Her eyes were pink around the lids.

"Is it all right if I go right now?" Sally was poised like the kite waiting for a breeze.

"Don't see why not," said Grandma. "Get my purse. You can buy a postcard to send your fam'ly and mail it at the post office. Stop by the shop and see if Sam'tha has an errand in need of doing."

Sally got Grandma's purse and hovered near as she figured out what sum to give her. "A penny for the stamp, and those colored postcards cost more than they ought. Well. Here's ten cents. Bring back the change."

"Thank you," said Sally. She flew out the driveway and began to skip down the long hill. The freedom offered by Cottersville was splendid. She wondered what they were doing at home . . . camping in the tent in the backyard and still coughing, poor things.

In the meadow below the Pine Grove there were

campions and Queen Anne's lace and black-eyed Susans. Sally waded into the long grass and picked a bouquet for the shop. Farther on, dawdling, she admired the cottage and its garden at the corner of Clemens Hill and Main. She was wondering if she dared reach over the fence to add a few larkspurs to her wild bouquet, when a bicycle bell and a bright voice, almost in her ear, made her jump.

"Did I scare you?" Evie said. She hopped off a sky-blue bicycle, so shiny it must have just been bought. It had balloon tires and a wire basket attached by leather straps to the handlebars. The sun caught on the curve of the chrome and glowed tiny fires. "Isn't this the cat's pajamas?"

"You have a new bike," Sally said, then let her eyes slide past Evie's to the bow in her hair. The bow was blue and silver to match the bicycle.

Evie frowned at a thumbprint on her handlebars. She breathed on it and rubbed it away with the tie of her middy blouse.

Searching for something to say, Sally remembered to mention, "You left the barrette from Aunt Samantha's in the car the other day. I have it at home."

"Did I forget that? I must have. I'll get it next time I come up. Wasn't it fun making tarts?" Evie grinned mischievously, then offered, "Want to try my bike? Say, *can* you ride a two-wheeler?"

Stung, Sally said, "Of course I can ride. I've ridden

since I was six!"

"Don't get mad," Evie said. "Lots of kids in my apartment house don't know how. My father rented this one downtown before he went back to the store. He's in the city for a couple days. Try it."

While Sally had had the whooping cough, her parents would not even let her move her bike from the garage. She had not had her toes on bicycle pedals since June. Now she yearned to try this beauty. One ride was not going to commit her to undying friendship. "I've ridden a bike for years and years," Sally said, not wanting to show her haste to ride. She kept her tone as offhand as she could make it.

"So, try it."

Sally slipped onto the leather seat and pedaled up the hill toward Aunt Samantha's. Breathless, knees trembling, she gave up halfway, wobbled around in the middle of the hill and then turned back. At least she managed to skid to a standstill in front of Evie by jamming hard on the coaster brakes. "The seat's too low for me," said Sally. Then, with more honesty, "I guess I'm out of practice." She lingered, reluctant to step out of her place behind the brilliant handlebars.

"Tell you what. We'll share. You can ride *me* on the back, and I'll ride *you*." Evie's eyes shone behind her glasses.

They took turns finding new places to ride each other. When they bumped across the hotel lawn, a woman who Evie whispered was Mrs. Grossman came out and asked them to stay off the grass. As she returned to the lobby, Evie said, "So's your old man," and clutched Sally around the waist where it tickled. Both laughing, they tumbled into a scratchy privet hedge. They sat on the grass by the fallen bike, and Sally helped Evie pull leaves out of her bow.

After another fit of giggles, Evie said, "I'm tired of riding, aren't you? It must be time for lunch. Stay for lunch with me. You will, won't you?"

"I forgot, I was going downtown," said Sally. The wild bouquet had gone limp in Evie's bike basket. Where had the morning gone? Sally was amazed. How could she have let her magic morning of freedom be frittered away while she rode and talked and laughed with a mere summer visitor? But in her heart of hearts, Sally knew that this morning had been one of the best times she'd had so far in Cottersville. She had not truly *liked* this girl before. Did she like her now? Sally gave Evie a slight frown.

"Come meet my mama," said Evie. "She likes me to have friends for lunch. She'll say stay, if I ask." Evie reached for Sally's hand. Abandoning the bicycle on the lawn where it had fallen, she tugged Sally into the lobby so that she could call Grandma from the desk telephone. Grandma told her lunch was fine, and she'd see her later.

When she hung up, Evie was nowhere in sight. Sally stood and gazed around her. She found she was facing a large bulletin board, placarded with notices and posters.

60

Some were printed, others handwritten. Sally read:

> *ONEG SHABAT*
> *Tascha Seidle & His Singing Violin*
> *In the Ballroom*   *5t*
> *After Services*

She had never heard of anything called "Oneg Shabat."
Imagine having a ballroom, though! Other signs caught
her attention:

STUART KOHN

VISITING CHESS MASTER

TEST YOUR SKILL

TUESDAY EVENING

> *Coming . . .*
> *Saturday Evening Next*   **3**
> *In the Dell (Ballroom in case of rain)*
> *THE ILLUSTRIOUS KOPINSKY TRIO*
> *Playing Works of Mozart, Handel, Beethoven*

Sally speculated, awed by the thought of Mozart,
Handel, and Beethoven being played in a vacation hotel.
When the Moffats went on vacation, her father fished;
her mother sat on the beach, and Sally and her brothers
squabbled over who rowed the tub of a rowboat. There
was no music besides the birds.

Evie returned. "What kind of a place *is* this?" Sally
said and pointed to the posters: "Some kind of school?"

"It's culture, silly. Come meet my mother."

"Culture?" Sally frowned. "Like cultured pearls?"

"You're kidding," said Evie. She hustled Sally out a

corridor toward another part of the hotel. "Mama's at the end of a reading."

Sally's teacher often read to her class on Friday afternoon. Sally imagined someone reading to a bunch of mothers. What? Newspapers? . . . Cookbooks? "What do they read?" she finally asked Evie.

"Poetry. It's a club." Evie was impatient. "Hurry up. She wants to go to lunch. We can eat with her today because it's only lunch, and you're a guest."

"Who do you eat with, I mean usually, when you have lunch?"

"Children. Children eat at the children's table. Stop here." Evie caught Sally by her tie belt. They had left the mahogany lobby and walked along a porch open on two sides. It connected the main hotel with what Sally guessed must be the ballroom. Evie stopped where the porch swelled out in an octagonal gazebo with railed seats and rolled bamboo shades. A dozen women were sitting there.

Evie pushed Sally ahead. "Here's Sally Moffat. This is my mama, Mrs. Grauber."

Evie's mother did not look like a mother. A movie star, Dolores Del Rio, maybe. Mrs. Grauber's hair, dark like Evie's, was sleek and short and swung forward in curves over her cheeks. She wore bright pink lipstick and pearl-button earrings. She had been painting her fingernails with a brush stuck into a tiny bottle of red lacquer. Mrs. Moffat had never done that. Neither would she have appeared in public in Mrs. Grauber's ripply, flowered beach pajamas. There was a series of bracelets on Mrs. Grauber's arms, and a diamond flashed as she waved her hand to dry her nails. "I'm so glad Evie brought a friend." Her voice was sweet.

Something snapped to inside Sally. The years of Mrs. Moffat's drilling in manners and in what was expected of children caught up with her. She extended her right hand to Mrs. Grauber, held her skirt out wide, and bowed low in her very best dancing-school curtsey.

"Chahming," said Evie's mother.

Evie squealed. "How did you do that? Teach me!" She grabbed Sally around the waist and waltzed her around. "I never saw anybody do that. Only in the newsreels for a queen once." Sally blushed. She guessed that she would not say that she had never seen anyone like Evie's mother except in the movies.

"A little *shiksa*," murmured one of the poetry readers. Sally wondered what *that* word meant. It did not sound like something one would enjoy.

"This is my friend, Sally Moffat," Evie said to the group. "She's visiting her grandmother who lives at the top of the road."

One or two of the women nodded and smiled at Sally, but as a whole they did not seem very welcoming. Sally was glad that Evie took her off to wash her hands before lunch. Sally asked, "What's that word that woman said? Shik-something?"

"Oh, you know. You're not Jewish. You're a gentile.

An outsider. Don't pay any attention to *her*," said Evie.
Sally wiped her hands on a towel of white hucking that
had "Grossman's Hotel" sewn into the hem with blue
thread. Here was Sally Moffat in Grossman's Hotel, and
her father did not approve of such places. Sally decided
to put her father out of her mind.

"Slowpoke!" said Evie in the doorway. "Let's go eat.
I'm hungry."

The hotel dining room was elegant. It had green
wallpaper and many round, white-clothed tables. There
were more knives and forks than Sally was used to, and
the linen napkins were as big as blankets. She took a sip
of water from a dazzling cut-glass goblet. Her eyes reg-
istered everything.

Sally was served a plate of red soup. She watched
Evie put a blob of whipped cream on hers. Whipped
cream was for puddings. Sally refused it. "You *have* to,"
said Evie and scooped up a spoonful for her. "It's sour
cream. You have it with borscht."

Mrs. Moffat threw out sour cream. Sally steeled her
stomach. She tested the soup with the tip of her tongue.
It was so icy cold it must be on purpose. She swallowed
some. The soup was tart *and* sweet, spicy even. Grandma
would have approved.

When their soup plates were empty, a waitress
brought in clean ones and a large, silvery covered platter containing small, rolled-up cylinders lying side by
side. Evie bounced on her chair. "I love blintzes, don't

64

you?" Evie helped herself to two of them and smothered them with more sour cream. She then sprinkled sugar on top liberally. Sally was served two also.

Curious about this other new food on her plate, Sally prodded one with her fork. "Blintzes? Are they like pigs-in-a-blanket?" Sometimes her mother wrapped a frank-furter in biscuit dough and baked it. It was called that.

Mrs. Grauber smiled at Sally. "Not likely," she said. "Mrs. Grossman keeps a kosher kitchen."

Sally knew she'd made some kind of error and felt dumb and gauche. She'd have to ask Evie about kosher later. She did not want Mrs. Grauber to think her stupid. Sally cut into her blintz. Cottage cheese oozed out, steaming hot. *Cold* soup and *hot* cheese. Good grief.

Evie, talking around bites, cleaned her plate in no time at all. She picked up crumbs and stuffed them into her mouth. Her mother said, "If you don't stop eating so much, you won't fit any of your clothes. You're a *fresser*, like your father."

"Kosher." Now "fresser." Sally was becoming aware of a language that was not hers. Its foreignness was as ap-pealing as the beauty of Mrs. Grauber. Curiosity got the better of her. "Please, what's a 'kosher' and a 'fresser'?"

While Mrs. Grauber looked amused, Evie said, "Not *a* kosher, just kosher. Don't you know Yiddish when you hear it? Mama means I'm a big eater, a fresser, like my papa. Kosher means it's okay for Jews to eat because it's blessed by the rabbi, see? Mama, can I have the last blintz? If Sally doesn't want it?"

65

Mrs. Grauber shrugged her shoulders in a way that Sally longed to practice. It seemed to signal that Evie's appetite was too much for Mrs. Grauber to bear, but she would gracefully let nature take its course. Sally wanted to try that shrug at home, when her mother used some of her "what would the neighbors think" stuff.

Mrs. Grauber pushed her chair away from the table. She wiped her mouth and left a line of pink on the napkin. She dropped the napkin on her chair when she rose. "I'm going to have coffee in the card room."

"But I want dessert!" protested Evie.

"So stay," said Mrs. Grauber. She flowed away in her swirling pajamas.

After her mother left, Evie ate a slice of molasses cake with hard sauce spread on it. Golly, this girl had a kind of a piggy appetite. Then she remembered that Evie had hesitated over Mr. Vanderdonck's baloney. "Is it that baloney isn't kosher?" she asked.

Evie licked her fork clean. "Yeah. I mean, you're not *supposed* to. Why didn't you order dessert? I could've eaten it for you."

Plain old greed, Sally thought. "Why aren't you supposed to eat baloney?" she persisted.

Evie threw down her fork, and it clattered on the empty plate. "I *told* you. Meat has to come from the right animals, and the rabbi has to say prayers over them, and Moses wrote it in the Bible. My father says they're five-thousand-year-old health rules." Evie rubbed her mouth on the napkin. "Do you like Matzo ball soup?"

"I never had any," Sally said. "You mean they're rules like brush your teeth before you go to bed, and wash your hands before you eat?" Sally's mother often said that cleanliness was next to godliness.

Evie giggled. "Yeah, and cover your mouth when you yawn and sneeze only in your handkerchief."

Sally's lips began to twitch into a grin. All the rules her anxious mother had given her so often bubbled up in her head like fizz in a glass of ginger ale. She said, "Say Good morning to the neighbors and Fine thank you when they ask how you are even if you're terrible. Never wipe your nose on your sleeve. Don't pick your nose in public, and don't scream loud in the street because what will the neighbors think." Her list sounded like a song: "Take care of your little brothers and hold their hands crossing the street. And never, *never* sit on the seat of a public toilet."

Evie burst into laughter. "You're so funny. I think kosher is more important because it's religious." She tipped her chair forward. "Listen, let's go try on Mama's dresses."

"Oughtn't we to ask first?"

"Poo," said Evie. "Kind of a goody-goody, aren't you? Come on." She pushed Sally out of the dining room.

They went to the broad flight of stairs in the lobby and headed upward. Their feet sank into the hotel's thickly carpeted treads. Evie opened a door in the up-

67

stairs corridor. "We'll try on *my* clothes. You won't get bothered by that. This is my room." It was easy to see that the room belonged to Evie. Most of the dresser drawers stuck out, teetering out of their grooves. Socks hung from a chair; a dozen hair bows of many colors littered a bedside table. The closet was already open. Evie dove in. "Try this one first." She handed a smart green plaid dress to Sally. "Hurry so I can see."

Sally unbuttoned her front buttons and held her arms up. Evie pulled the dress she was wearing over her head. That left Sally exposed, in bloomers and her cotton undershirt. She realized Evie was staring at her gold locket that had been hidden under her dress. It was a birthday present, from a year ago, from Aunt Samantha. The locket was one of Sally's prize possessions.

Evie seized the locket on its chain. "How pretty!" she said. "I *love* lockets. Wish I had one like this. Can you open it?"

Sally pressed the side of the locket with her thumbnail. Inside was a picture of Plush, and a lock of his black-and-white fur. "How cuckoo! It's a *dog*. Can I try it on?"

"You'd ask for anything," Sally said.

Evie's eyes creased with amusement at herself. "That's what my father says." She strung the locket around her neck and made double chins trying to see how it hung. "Do you think I'm getting bosoms?"

Secretly wishing her own collar bones were not so near the surface, Sally said, "You're just fat."

Evie leaned to look in her mirror inside the closet door. "Fat? Well, but I think they're growing." She tried squeezing her elbows into her chest. She examined her profile. "There *are* bumps," she said

Sally ignored Evie. She tried on the green plaid dress, but it didn't fit.

Evie went back to pushing dresses this way and that. She selected one and flapped it at Sally. "Here's what I was looking for. My uncle sent it from Paris, only the size isn't right for me. Try it on. Blue's your color." The dress was real velvet, cut princess style, with a square neckline and high puffed sleeves. "Put it on, dear. I think it's for you."

Recognizing Evie's salesgirl voice, Sally let her help with the hooks.

She studied herself in the long mirror. The dress actually looked grand. The blue of the velvet and the blue of her eyes were the same. The lines of the dress might have been molded to her slimness. Only in her dreams had she appeared so elegant.

"Take it home," said Evie. "That's absolutely the cat's meow on you. Gorgeous."

Sally swallowed and avoided her eyes in the mirror. "Oh, I couldn't." Greed was sinful. She started to undo the hooks. What would people think if she went home with a gift from *Paris*? She could not do that. She stroked the fabric. It was so rich and soft.

"It's your dress," said Evie.

"You can't give away your clothes," said Sally. She

69

took the dress off and carefully laid it on the bed.

"Sure I can. You give me your locket, and I'll give you the dress. That's even Steven, isn't it?"

Sally stamped her foot. "I *can't* give away the locket. Aunt Samantha gave it to me. You ought not to give away your uncle's gift either." Swiftly, she changed back into her old cotton.

Evie unhooked the locket and handed it to Sally. She was not disturbed. "You can have the dress anyway. I thought you'd like to trade. If you feel better, we'll ask Mama."

Sally's hand closed on the hem of that soft material. She was definitely covetous. Greedy. She ought not to feel that way. How she hated Evie for making her feel grasping, when she knew it was wrong. "I don't want your dress," Sally burst out. She ran out the door of Evie's room and down the stairs. At the landing, she shouted, "Thanks for lunch."

Feeling foolish to be passionately running away, Sally ran through the lobby and down the porch steps. Free and clear of temptation, on the Clemens Hill pavement, she finally slowed down. She was determined that she would *not* have anything to do with that Evie ever again.

Chapter VII

Sally was sitting on her window seat, dreaming of a princess in blue velvet, when she heard Uncle Packer call from the foot of the stairs. "Sally? You up there?"

"I'm here." One leg had been folded under too long, and it prickled as she limped to the landing and leaned over the rail. Something was up. She could tell from Uncle Packer's hat. He was wearing his blue volunteer fireman's cap with gold braid across the visor. He was a Chief Emeritus.

"I have a batch of tickets for the bake. Come help me cover the town," Uncle Packer said. *That* was it, the Annual Firemen's Benefit Picnic, called more often "the bake." It was a Cottersville main event, held toward the end of August. To sell tickets they'd walk up and down Main Street, in and out of shops. Sally had gone with

Uncle Packer last year. She'd gotten cheese at the grocer's and home-made chocolates at the confectioner's.

"Oh boy," she said. "Do we start right now?"

"Yes. Smarten up a bit." Sally changed her shorts for a skirt and brushed at her hair. She took the stairs two at a time. Out front, Uncle Packer was starting the car. Aunt Samantha had left it for him today. He shouted out the window, "Early bird gets best pickings. Let's hustle, girlie."

As Uncle Packer slowed down at Grossman's Mountain House for the turn into Main, Sally leaned out her window. She inspected the rockers. No Mrs. Grauber. No Evie, even. One woman with gray hair waved and smiled at her. Sally waved in return. She wasn't sure, this morning, whether she hated Evie or not. The hotel had its fascinations. Sally wondered if "the illustrious Kopinsky trio" played the "Three O'Clock in the Morning" waltz. She might ask Evie. *If* she ever visited her again, that is.

They parked in the weedy yard behind Aunt Samantha's shop. They did not go in, only waved at her through the window. They walked to where State Route 189 ended, and the proper Main Street began. Sally followed Uncle Packer into the coolness of Heinemann's Pharmacy.

"Good morning, George," said Uncle Packer.

"Say, 'tis," said the pharmacist. He came out from behind his counter. "Sally? Haven't seen you since last year. Have a phosphate?"

"Yes, thank you," said Sally. She climbed onto one of the stools at the soda counter.

Mr. Heinemann rubbed his chin. "Don't know where that deuced boy is. I told him to be here by half past nine." He started through the counter gate.

Uncle Packer caught him by the tail of his jacket. "Whoa, George. Let Sally help herself. I got these new pumpers for you to look at. We got to figure which we buy after we make the rest of the money from the bake."

"Sure. Be careful with that carbonation faucet, Sally. It's got a lot of power . . . blow your drink sky-high if you use it too fast."

Sally was ready to explode like the faucet. To have her choice of rows of shiny handles and gobs of syrupy dips! She hurried through the gate. Would Sam and Colin be green!

Sally's hand hovered over the ordinary tumblers, the kind Mr. Heinemann used for phosphates. It would be too bad to waste this once-in-a-lifetime chance on the nikel glasses. Sally glanced toward Uncle Packer and Mr. Heinemann. They had a catalogue open between them and were talking almost chin to chin. She moved to the monster glasses, footed and fluted like Greek pillars. She placed one under the spigot labeled "Lime" and gave the handle a short squeeze. Lemon, she thought, went so nicely with lime. Some lemon then. She added a generous squeeze of cherry. Golly, but the squeezing and shooting in of flavors was scrumptious. She might as well squeeze them all. Orange. Caramel. Sarsaparilla. Now, some pineapple sundae topping, oh boy, and how could she skip the strawberry? Anything she'd missed?

It was time for the carbonated water. There wasn't much room. She remembered to be very careful and eased the faucet so foam barely oozed over the rim of her glass. She stirred and tasted. A mix of essences rolled along her tongue. The color turned muddy. Sally got a straw, but it clogged on chopped strawberries.

She took the straw out and drank more deeply. Her concoction had an interesting flavor . . . in a way. Actually, the mixture was . . . rather intense. She drank again. Ugh, it was sweet and heavy, too sickeningly sticky. She chewed a fragment of pineapple. More carbonation might help, but the glass was still too full.

"You work here? I want a small orangeade with lots of ice." A boy about Sam's age crouched on a stool with his elbows on the counter.

Relieved from the chore of drinking, Sally abandoned her glass. "That's a nickel." Feeling quite superior behind the counter, she plunged a small tumbler into the crushed ice, lifted it with a flourish, added a squirt of Orange—and squeezed the carbonation faucet. *Phphphphphttt.* She sprayed a cloud of fizz water and orange over both of them. Sally froze.

The boy sneezed. "Wish *I* could do that." He rubbed splatters from his forehead and licked his hand. "You got

74

foam in your hair."

Sally stole a glance across the store. Mr. Heinemann seemed not to be bothered. Uncle Packer folded his catalogue. "Now about the bake. How many tickets you need this year?"

"Four's sufficient," said Mr. Heinemann. He winked at Sally. "Leastwise, *some* of us know our own limits." Sally was glad her enormous tumbler was below the counter. She tipped it into the sink.

On the way out, Uncle Packer held the door open for her. "Be sure to come again," said Mr. Heinemann. "I always welcome a good appetite. 'This little pig went to market,' oink-oink." He chuckled, richly amused. "Hahaha. Hope you didn't try the bitters flavor." He *was* making fun of her for being so piggy, but how did he *know?*

Cross because her greed had been discovered, Sally enjoyed the morning less than she'd expected. The cheese at the grocer's was too sharp. The chocolate she was offered at the confectioner's was a brazil-nut nougat, and Sally hated brazil nuts. When they left the last place, a lawyer's office were there was nothing to eat at all, Sally saw that a cloud had passed over the morning's brilliant sun. "Thunderhead. There's a storm brewing," said Uncle Packer. "Best get home before it pours."

"It's only one cloud." Sally felt perverse. When they rounded the corner to Clemens Hill, she immediately had an idea. "Stop, Uncle Packer, stop!" He was startled enough to jam the brakes on hard. They jolted forward.

"What's up, girlie? Dog I didn't see?"

They were directly opposite Grossman's Mountain House. "The families at the hotel," said Sally. "We ought to ask them to the picnic. You'd sell a lot of tickets there, in one place, Uncle Packer, better than us traipsing around downtown." She was already out of the car.

"It's going to rain any minute," said Uncle Packer. He squinted at the sky.

"We'll be *inside*. Please."

"F'Pete's sakes," grumbled Uncle Packer. "These people never come to village doings." Sally crossed the street. "All right. I'm coming."

Drops fat as quarters dotted the sidewalk as Sally raced up the porch steps, followed by Uncle Packer. There was a whoosh of breeze at her skirt as the storm let down in earnest behind them. Thunder crashed. The women and men who had been sitting on the porch hastily scraped their rocking chairs away from the beating rain. Someone said, "Come in and keep dry," and Sally and Uncle Packer crowded into the lobby with the rest.

"Some drencher you brought," said a familiar voice. Evie's father was there. So he'd returned from his trip to the city. Sally smiled at him. He was really very tall and so well dressed. He had a jeweled stickpin in his tie. It glowed purple when Mrs. Grossman switched on the lights. "How's the grandmama?" Mr. Grauber said. "Some lady she is."

76

Sally wanted him to meet Uncle Packer, but she'd lost him. At last she saw him in a shadowy corner by the umbrella stand. She had to squeeze through a group of people to pull him out. "We're selling tickets for the Annual Firemen's Benefit Picnic," she said to Mr. Grauber. "Tell him, Uncle Packer."

Uncle Packer had his chief's cap scrunched under his arm, and he seemed reluctant. "We don't want to ask strangers for money," he said into Sally's ear. "We can take care of our own."

What *was* he fretting about? "Anybody who wants to can buy tickets," she said. "You told Mr. Heinemann you need money to buy a new pumper."

"Aha," said Mr. Grauber. "Tell me too. We certainly want to help the Fire Department. They make the hotel safer for us. Hilda. . . ." He beckoned to Mrs. Grossman. "We are going to buy lots of tickets and get a new pumper and reduce your insurance rates." Mr. Grauber pulled at his upper lip. "Yes. That is it. Reduce insurance rates." He banged the bell on Mrs. Grossman's desk. "Your attention please." He placed an arm around Sally and drew her forward. "We got an opportunity to purchase tickets for the Fire Department's Benefit Picnic." He smiled at Sally. "This lovely young woman will pass among you. You have the tickets, sir?" Uncle Packer brought a packet out of his vest. Mr. Grauber fanned out a handful like playing cards and held them high so everybody could see. "Who's buying the first four? Frank?"

77

Mr. Grauber saw the chief's hat under Uncle Packer's arm. He put it on his own head and followed Sally to make change. Sally felt a pinch on her upper arm. "I love picnics," said Evie. "Isn't my father wonderful? People feel good buying from him." Since Uncle Packer was doing nothing at all to help, it was a good thing Mr. Grauber was so encouraging. Together, he and Sally sold the whole batch.

When they were on their way again, Sally noticed Uncle Packer looked as if he had sucked a lemon. To cheer him up, she said, "Look at the dollar bills, Uncle Packer. Did you ever sell so many tickets before?"

"Um," said Uncle Packer. "Don't know what the committee will say. We never had these people before. You know, vacationers—they're not exactly our kind of people."

"What's our kind of people?"

"Oh, well." Uncle Packer stuck a cigar into his mouth. "Samantha will enjoy them. She enjoys everybody."

"Yes, and Grandma," said Sally. "She's already met Evie's father."

But that evening Grandma turned stubborn and announced she would not go to the bake. "It's the first you ever missed, Mother," said Aunt Samantha. "Aren't you feeling well?"

"Feel good as new," snapped Grandma. She worked her teeth a bit. "It gets too hot on that firehouse lawn. Not enough shade."

"Aw," said Sally. Grandma must go. "I'll hold your parasol for you," she offered.

"Thank y'kindly," said Grandma. "Truth is, I can't chew those quahogs in the bake. My plate clacks. I always used to favor 'em so, it's a real disappointment to pass 'em up." She held up a thin, knotty hand. "No, don't coax, and don't tell me there's plenty else to eat. There's no point to my going when I can't eat my portion."

Sally said, "But we'd cut them up for you in teeny bits."

"Pap for babies," snorted Grandma. "Don't want to feel the toothless old woman I really am." She patted Sally's cheek, and then smiled her tender smile. "Don't fret and fuss. Have the grace to let me know my own mind."

Grandma was the only person Sally knew who could use a word like "grace" as if it were as everyday as "salt" or "sock" or "picnic." "Anyway, I'll miss you," said Sally.

"Nice to be missed," said Grandma.

The day of the Firemen's Picnic was, as Grandma predicted, a scorcher. Engine #1, COTTERSVILLE VOLUNTEER FIRE COMPANY, had been polished with hard wax and shone hot as fire as it came down Main Street. The Drum and Bugle Corps led the way, fourteen men and the boy who helped balance the bass drum. Behind the Corps came the Fire Company. Uncle Packer was splendid in a black jacket with epaulets and his gold-

79

encrusted cap. There were no horses. For a moment, Sally remembered the parade of earlier summer, how she had been awed to gooseflesh at the eeriness of the masked marchers. Here everything was blithe and easy. She left the curb to run beside a pack of children on decorated bicycles. She was going to meet Evie after the parade on the firehouse lawn. Then all of them were to eat together at table 8. It had been arranged by Aunt Samantha on the phone with Mrs. Grauber. Sally was quite excited. She had pushed any distress she had ever felt about Evie into some far corner of her mind.

By the time she arrived at the picnic grounds behind the firehouse, the engine was already parked, and children were climbing up to its black-leather seat. Bunting decorated the open stalls that had been set up outside, and the American flag had been raised on its pole. A trickle of smoke drifted over the green lawn and white-draped tables. The barbecue fires and the baking pit were tended at the rear of the firehouse.

Sally's throat was dry from running, so she stopped at the lemonade booth. It fluttered with red, white, and blue banners and had a tarpaulin roof to shade the ice from the sun. "Please," she said, and unknotted a quarter, contributed by Aunt Samantha, from the corner of her handkerchief, "may I have a small glass?"

She folded the change into the handkerchief again and surveyed the scattered crowd as she sipped her lemonade. The pies-and-cakes booth, three tables angled together, displayed nothing yet, but women in matching red-checked aprons were opening boxes and baskets of donations.

Bang! She jumped. A small firecracker had exploded at her feet. There was loud snickering from some honeysuckle bushes nearby. She pretended to pull up her socks and not notice. Some kids always managed to save a few firecrackers from the Fourth of July for the bake. It was a nuisance.

"Hey, Sally!" Sally turned. Her eyes widened. It was Evie, dressed in a blaze of color. She was coming over the lawn alone, so her father must be parking the car in the parking lot across the street. Sally blinked in envy. Evie wore a crimson, or maybe it was fire-engine red, dress, and a bow printed with blue and white stars pinned into her hair.

"They oughta run her up a flagpole," said a boy's voice in the bushes.

"Watch out!" yelled Sally. A firecracker kicked up dust in front of Evie. *Bang!*

Evie stopped and thumbed her nose at the honeysuckle. "I know where you're at, scaredy cat," she hollered. "Hey, Sally, show me where everything gets cooked and everything. I've never been to a firemen's picnic before.

They set out together to see the fire truck. The black leather smelled fragrant in the heat, and the bell clanged when Evie pulled its rope. "Pretty spiffy," said Evie. "What's next?"

They joined the crowd of people watching and waiting at the cooking grounds. There were two spits where spareribs were turning, but the glory of the picnic, Sally felt, was the pit where the combination food bags were steaming. The bags were made of hard twine netting, and each held a half chicken, a sweet potato, a sausage, and a dozen clams. The clams were the special treat of the Firemen's Picnic. They were ordered by rail and sent to West Kill in barrels of ice. Lindsay's Ice van trucked them to Cottersville. Sally wanted to be at the pit when the bags of food were taken out. "How come they don't burn up?" asked Evie.

"You'll see," said Sally. "It's the way they're steamed."

They arrived just in time. Two firemen, sleeves rolled to the elbow, shoveled aside layers of curling cornhusks. It was a hot job. They had already unpacked a layer of glowing coals, and their red suspenders were sweated dark at the back. Evie smacked her lips. "It smells ter-iff-ic, but what's the garbage on top?"

The nearest fireman raised his eyebrows. He bristled at Evie. He'd probably been working since six in the morning. "Guess you never been to a bake before," he said. "That's corn shucks and seaweed to keep the heat in. So the coals don't singe what you're going to eat." He leaned on his shovel and examined Evie from her starry bow to her clean white shoes. "New around here?"

"She's *my friend* from the hotel," said Sally, emphasizing the words on purpose. "Grossman's Mountain House Hotel, down the hill from Aunt Samantha's." Sally thought he murmured "one of those," but she decided not to stay and watch further. It was time to eat. "Those bags are cool enough to touch now. Let's find our table."

They chose two dripping bags of food and made their way to Table 8. A woman with a red arm band pointed the way. She also brought them a pitcher of ice water. "You're the first here," she said. "I'll bring the corn and the butter pots after the table's full."

Sally poured water for them both and could hardly wait to get to the food in front of her. Evie, she saw out of the corner of her eye, was acting funny. When she had spilled her bag open in front of her, she went rigid. Her hands pushed against the rim of the table. Sally turned and stared. Evie had a very odd pinch to her lips. She whispered, "They're *looking* at me."

"Who?" Sally stopped gnawing at a drumstick and swung her head from side to side. It wasn't like Evie to be shy of someone.

"Them." Evie did not remove her hands from the table edge, but she pointed with one finger. The clams lay, gape-shelled, between her knife and fork.

"The clams?" Sally laughed. "They're *cooked*. They've been cooking since early this morning." She watched Evie separate the clams, with her paper napkin, from the rest of the meal. She swiveled the shells so they faced the other way. "Silly," said Sally. "They're delicious. You tip them into your mouth. Try like this." She pried a shell farther apart and grabbed the quahog with her teeth. Ummm. Lovely. She swallowed. "Then you nibble off the ears. . . ."

Evie gasped. "The ears!"

"They aren't really. They're the little part at the side that holds the clam shut when they're out in the ocean." Sally sucked at a shell. "They're its muscles, I guess."

"Don't say any more," said Evie. She shoved the clams at Sally with the edge of her knife. "I saw crabs walking sidewise at Atlantic City."

"These aren't crabs. They're quahogs. Clams."

Evie held her hands over her own ears. "Don't tell me about them."

Sally grinned. Stupid Evie to be afraid of a clam. Sally felt an enormous sense of power. "*Eat* it," she said. She thrust a large open shell under Evie's nose. Evie averted her face. Dumb summer visitor. "It's good. Look." The plump clam, rippled and pinky brown, sat steaming in its shell. "*Smell* it. Go *on*." Evie lifted her shoulder away and gave a whimper of distaste.

" 'Have the grace to let me know my own mind.' "

Sally gave a start. It was Grandma's voice, but Grandma had not come to the picnic. It was as if Grandma had spoken inside Sally's head, clear as clear. Sally dropped the clam. It rolled off the table. She ducked her head and hunted for it in the trampled grass. She felt a little sick at her own violence. Grandma would never deliberately hurt someone that way. Even though Evie had insisted she try sour cream and hot cheese it was no excuse.

Sally said, "You can have my chicken, okay? And I'll

have your clams." She made the exchange. "When they bring the corn, you want to share a butter pot with me?" Evie nodded. The two girls ate silently, in unspoken companionship.

The Graubers arrived, with much laughter and talk, and sat down on either side of them. Sally noticed they had sweet potatoes and barbecued chicken halves, but none of the steamed bags of clams and sausage.

Then Aunt Samantha and Uncle Packer came. Everyone had to shake hands. Aunt Samantha, as usual, was talky and flighty, and became absorbed with Mr. Grauber's talk about business trends. Uncle Packer chewed clams glumly until Mrs. Grauber asked about his Fire Chief's hat. Then he got to reminiscing about fires he had presided over. When he told his funny story about rescuing old Mrs. Stillman, who insisted on getting on her best dressing gown before being carried down the ladder, Sally knew that he was enjoying himself after all. Mrs. Grauber had an especially nice, throaty laugh when she was amused.

Sally was glad they were all together. Except, of course, they weren't all together because Grandma was at home. Sally sighed and put down her second ear of corn.

"Too much of the good things to eat?" said Mrs. Grauber.

"I was thinking about my grandmother," said Sally. "You could have met her if she were here."

"Maybe she can come for tea in the afternoon," said Mrs. Grauber. "I will call and invite her, shall I?" She smiled at Sally. There was a dimple in one cheek when she smiled. Her tan silk dress, Sally thought, set off her dark hair and eyes in an unusual way. "Does next Monday seem all right?"

"I'll ask," said Sally. "I'm sure Grandma would like that."

"I will telephone."

"That is very gracious of you," said Sally. Funny she should use that word. Something about Mrs. Grauber gave Sally a need to be very polite. Grandma, with her sharp intuition, could explain why this was. Grandma would *know*.

Mrs. Grauber said, "I am looking forward to Monday already."

"Me too," said Evie.

CHAPTER VIII

Nobody bothered much with supper that evening. "Stuffed full as a mule in a melon patch," said Uncle Packer. He was stretched out on the wicker couch on the sun porch. Grandma sat close by a west window to get the last of the light. She was tatting lace with little ebony bobbins that whisked in and out. Aunt Samantha had gone to the sewing room. The *clackety-clack* of her machine filled the house with a comfortable hum. "It worked out better than I thought it might," said Uncle Packer.

"What worked out?" asked Grandma.

"Those people from the hotel that came to the bake . . . I thought somebody might object." Uncle Packer undid his belt a notch and sighed with relief.

"Doesn't seem to me these vacationers object to the

97

village, elsewise they wouldn't come," said Grandma. Sally saw her grandmother's lip quirk. She was deliberately misunderstanding Uncle Packer, just to tease.

He shifted on his cushions till his feet were higher than his head. "You're pulling my leg, Mother Byrd."

Grandma pushed at the cretonne curtains a bit. "Need more *light* in here," she said.

Uncle Packer chuckled. "I know when I'm cornered. I'm talking about people *here* objecting. City folks . . . they've never come to a picnic before. Kept to themselves." Sally thought she heard Grandma's teeth go *clack*. "Yep," said Uncle Packer, "now it seems they're all over town. Lots of the women wear pants. Too much lipstick. I've seen 'em in shorts in the bank. Bare legs. In the *bank*."

"Uncle Packer," said Sally, "when I grow up, I am going to wear plenty of lipstick and own tons of beach pajamas and about a million shorts. And wear them in the bank, if I want to."

"Hmmmp-hmmmp," went Grandma. Sally wondered which kind of noise she'd make if she knew about her trying to push that clam in Evie's face. Sally decided not to tell her. She was not exactly proud of her moment of feeling mean.

She said instead, "You talked a long time to Evie's mother, Uncle Packer. *She* didn't have bare legs. Did you notice?"

"Say now, she's a real stunner," said Uncle Packer. "I

88

didn't mean her. And that Grauber seems all right. Except his speech at the end about how they'd enjoyed the bake and hoped we could do this every year—well—there you are. Give an inch and they take a mile."

"I thought he was saying a nice thank-you," said Sally.

"We used to have the higher types, though. The literary gents and ladies . . . actresses like Maude Adams . . . writers like Mark Twain."

Grandma said, "You say that now, Packer, but *I* remember folks used to complain the actors gave wild parties and the writer fellas drank like fish. I'd know." Grandma folded up her lace and bobbins. "Seems to me you're giving the child folderol notions, Packer. *Higher* types. Higher than what? Hmmmp." Grandma tucked the lace in a bag and tied its strings tight. She looked at Sally. "It's time to put a body into perspective. Let's have our picnic at Stone Bridge tomorrow."

Sally dropped the pieces of jigsaw puzzle she had been working at and hugged Grandma's thin shoulders. "That's the cat's pajamas," she said.

To Sally, Stone Bridge was as special a place as Grandma was a person. Stone Bridge was not so much a bridge as a vast wall of rock, under which a stream simply sank, disappeared. The hollow where the Bridge rose, in the middle of a forest, was so tumbled with huge boulders and so noisy with the rush of waters that Sally felt small and unimportant. There all was mysterious, and Sally became part of the mystery.

In anticipation of the trip, Sally was up next morning early. She helped prepare lunch and a bigger jug of lemonade than usual because a visit to Stone Bridge was a long affair. After breakfast, Aunt Samantha drove them as far as the old logging road at the beginning of the forest. "Packer will pick you up at four," she said. Sally grabbed the basket of lunch, heavy with sandwiches and pie, and galloped into the pines. She jumped from rut to rut of the path, and set the basket covers flapping. It was so good to be able to run without whooping. Swift as a deer, she felt.

Grandma settled a shawl around her shoulders. "Fasten the lids on that basket," she called. "You'll feed our lunch to the rest of God's creatures."

Sally slowed down. The pines grew so tall and thick that darkness had closed around her. Branches arched far above, and ahead was an endless march of tree trunks. There was not a sound. Not a bird twittered. Sally looked around. "Who's here besides us—bears?"

"Always something living under a root or behind a bush."

Sally waited for Grandma to catch up. There was a lonesome feel to so much forest space. "Even a rabbit wouldn't live in here—it's so dark."

Grandma reached out to help Sally carry the basket. "When I was your age, I thought the forest was churchly, so maybe the rabbits come only on Sunday. And the bears. All God's creatures make up the church of the world." Grandma did not go hmmmp-hmmmp, so she must be serious. As Sally walked along, she could understand why Grandma might think of the forest as "churchly." The fallen needles muffled their footsteps, made them walk as quietly as if they were in church.

In front of them a sunbeam struck through the gloom. The pines were thinning out. Sally listened. She could hear the roaring of the waters as they dashed themselves against the rocks and the cliff. It was like shouting, far off. "I hear it," she said. "That's the Caspar Kill."

"Who's to say what you hear?" said Grandma. "Voices in the wilderness, seems to me. See the sun ladder?" She pointed to the sunbeam, scattered with dust motes. "Reminds me of the story of Jacob's ladder. Angels are there, if we could only see 'em, climbing up and down." Sally narrowed her eyes at Grandma. Her face was grave, and she still did not say hmmmp-hmmmp.

"There aren't any such things as angels," said Sally. "You've never seen any."

"No," said Grandma, "but then, grandchild, I've never seen a whale. Or an ocean liner. But I know they're there."

Sometimes Grandma was a puzzle. She said things that needed thinking about, and Sally did not want to think at all today, just run and run. She was in a hurry to see Stone Bridge. The babble of the current, growing louder in front of her, urged her on.

She emerged from the trees way ahead of Grandma.

The cliff reared itself in front of her, damp with spray. The Caspar Kill, fast roaring down the mountainside, rushed headlong into the granite wall, pummeled itself into spray, and formed rainbows in the sunshine. The mystery was that most of the water went underground and surfaced miles away, down the mountainside.

Sally placed the basket on an expanse of moss and walked to the water. She plunged her hand in the icy current, then pulled it out fast. Her fingers tingled. She stepped as close as she could to the spray that spurted up the cliff, and let the moisture wet her face and form droplets on the wool of her sweater. It was so chilly she felt as if she were in an icebox.

Grandma strolled onto the granite and looked into the moil of waters. "Can't make ourselves heard over that rambunctious fuss," she had to shout at Sally. "Let's move upstream."

"I want to find an island," said Sally, "something all my own I can wade to." She picked up the basket, and they wandered beside rocks as big as Sally, away from the noise and the cliff.

At last, Grandma paused at a table of granite, flat enough for serving lunch on. "Go 'long," she said. "I know you want to get wet before we eat. Time enough to dry out then. I'll get things ready."

Sally grinned and took off her shoes and socks. It was hard to step into that freezing water, but she had to do it each summer. She shuddered with the awful cold and went deeper in the stream.

Her feet scrunched over pebbles. Watching her toes wriggle in the clear water, Sally saw a pebble of garnet red. She picked it up. There was another, spotted green like a frog. She picked it up too, and a pink one, and another and another. Wading and collecting pebbles, Sally moved farther and farther away from Grandma. Her feet went numb. She had so many pebbles in her pockets that they bumped along her thighs, wet and heavy. Ouch, but her toes were icy knots. When she came to a big, dry chunk of boulder, Sally decided to climb out and warm herself.

She rubbed her feet and ankles and looked around. The water flowed on either side of her. She had found an island. There was a strip of glitter that ran across the middle. White quartz. It had a slickness different from the rough granite. She tried to pry out a sliver and broke a fingernail. A rosette of dandelion leaves was growing there. Pretty. The quartz stripe might be a huge necklace with the dandelion for a locket. Sally lay on the warm rock and shut her eyes. A necklace in the rock . . . a necklace for giants . . . or how about Grandma's angels?

Through the red-and-gold haze that seeped through her eyelids, Sally imagined a hand large enough to spread the rock apart and pluck the necklace. Then she thought of an arm big enough to go with the hand, and a neck to put the necklace around, and a . . . She caught her breath. The island moved! A cold wave of air pulsed over her.

Sally opened her eyes and jerked up, feeling goose-flesh on her spine. Something *had* been there, and she had not been quick enough to see. Something had set the dandelion nodding and bobbing on its stem. Quickly, she splashed ashore.

She ran along the rocky beach, heedless of bruises. "Grandma!" she called, louder than she had intended. It seemed as if she had been gone a very long time.

"Land, Sally," said Grandma. "What bunches up your pockets so?"

Grateful for the question, Sally turned her pebble collection into Grandma's lap. She sat close beside her; Grandma was so *real*. "Water stones," said Grandma. She rubbed the surfaces with her thumb. "Feel how smooth the water's made them." Sally liked the way her grandma held first one pebble and then another. "Hah," she said, looking into her hand. "Here's a different-shaped one. See how my thumb fits? Hold the stone and put your thumb just so." It was a pinkish stone, oblong, with a deep hollow in one side.

Sally held the stone with her thumb fitted into the place the water had made for it. Or suppose a giant had molded it, as easily as she molded clay at school. "It's a thumbstone," she said.

"Possibly so," said Grandma. She considered, very thoughtful. "Think how it's been rolling in that stream, knocking about, bumped smooth here, bumped smooth there. Guess I'd call it a friendstone. Hmmmp-hmmmp. Like friends get tumbled around with experience, hm? Till they fit together nice and comf'table."

Grandma expressed thoughts so well that Sally wanted to tell her about her island moving. There was some—well, poetry, in that, that Grandma would understand. But suppose she had only been dreaming, wide-awake, as her mother often complained?

Sally was aware of Grandma waiting, looking at her, gentle but rather inquisitive. How long had she been silent? She said, "That's how you and I are, Grandma, comfortable friends together."

"Naturally," said Grandma. "And now, I think it's time for lunch."

CHAPTER IX

"What shall we do with your stones, Sally?" asked Grandma after they had eaten.

"I want them," said Sally, "especially the friendstone one. I'll put them in the basket." Sally hoisted the basket onto her hip and trudged through the forest. At the highway, she sat on the wooden railing until Grandma joined her.

A horn tooted, *Hoo-gah, Hoo-gah.* "How are my two girlies?" said Uncle Packer as he got out of the car to take the picnic basket. "What's in there—lead?"

Sally was planning to arrange the stones on the shelves of the Fort. "What would you say if I told you rubies and emeralds?"

"Try me."

"Rubies and emeralds," said Sally.

Uncle Packer shoved the basket under his jacket.

96

"Hsst," he whispered. "Let's escape with the loot." Sally laughed and waited for Grandma to make some spicy comment.

Grandma seemed to be tired. She tried the step to the running board and missed three times. "Never mind the jewels, Packer, just hoist me up. I'm plumb weary this afternoon."

Uncle Packer tucked Grandma into the back seat. "Going to keep me company up front, Sally?" He put the basket on the floor and moved as if to help her up too.

Sally jumped in by herself. Her slacks were rolled up and she extended a leg toward Uncle Packer. "You mind if I go home with my knees showing, Uncle Packer? You said you didn't like bare legs in the village."

Uncle Packer tweaked her bare calf. "You think I'm a dotty old codger, *I* know," he said, "but wait till your daddy hears you've been hobnobbing at that hotel." He blew out his mustache at her and started the car.

Sally watched the trees slide by. She had not wanted to think of what her father might say about Grossman's Hotel. Feeling defensive, Sally remembered the interesting bulletin board. "The hotel is very educational. Do you know they have concerts and visiting chess masters?" she said.

"*Sssssssn-a-a-azzz-zz.*" There was a choked-off wheeze or snore in the rear seat. Sally turned around to see. "Grandma is sound asleep," she said.

So as not to wake Grandma, they spoke very little on

the ride back. At the top of Clemens Hill, Uncle Packer switched off the engine and let the car roll into the gravel drive by itself. "Brought the cook home safe and sound," he said. He got out and opened the back door with a flourish.

"Grandma's still asleep," said Sally. She hopped out with the basket of stones. She reached down to unroll her slacks. They had dried in accordion pleats.

"Mother Byrd," said Uncle Packer, "time to wake up." There was no answer. "Mother, we're home," said Uncle Packer. He reached inside the car and shook her gently. Grandma's eyes were closed, and her cheeks were sunken below her bones. As Uncle Packer tried to wake her, she slid down the leather upholstery until she was lying flat across the seat. Her legs were at an awkward angle to the rest of her body, and Sally expected her to complain about legs not being what they used to be.

Though Grandma's breathing was even, she did not waken. She reminded Sally of a puppet unstrung. Her petal skin looked as white as her hair. Uncle Packer cleared his throat and stared at the horizon. He took his unlighted cigar out of his mouth and put it in his vest pocket. Then, without meeting Sally's eyes, he said, "I'll call Samantha." He brushed his mustache with his thumb. "And I think Dr. Carlson. Stay with your grandmother." He climbed the steps to the sun porch and went into the house.

Sally's heart began to throb in her ears. The tone of Uncle Packer's voice frightened her. Suddenly she did not want to be near Grandma. It was an upsetting feeling. She wanted to run away. She sidled to the edge of the drive and clutched her elbows, arms tight over her middle. Grandma was not so frail that she needed a *doctor*. Sally's stomach shuddered.

How calm Grandma had been when Sally had been sick in the meadow, that first day. Sally wanted to be calm and helpful too. She returned to the car and whispered through the open door, "It's been a long day, Grandma. We walked awfully far. You're overtired, but you're going to be all right."

Huffing and puffing a little, Uncle Packer clattered down the back steps. "I called Samantha. She's getting a ride home." He closed the door on Grandma and got into the driver's seat. "We're lucky. The doctor was in. He's coming. In or out, Sally. I got to drive to the front of the house to get her inside."

Sally climbed in. Uncle Packer drove to the front walk. If he had to carry Grandma into the house, it was easier to do it from in front. "Shall I turn down Grandma's bed?" Sally said.

"That's a good girl," said Uncle Packer. "Prop the front door open."

Sally rushed up the one brick step of the front porch and opened the front door. The door stopper Aunt Samantha used was an antique flatiron. Sally shoved it into place and, without a glance at the living-room owl, turned into the back hall. She went directly into Grandma's neat room. The milking stool Grandma used for stepping into her high feather bed was on the rag rug next to it. She pushed the stool under the bed so no one would stumble over it. She drew back the seersucker spread and creased the sheets in an open triangle. There. The bed would welcome Grandma.

Uncle Packer was calling. What? Bring a chair, he was saying. Sally picked up a rush-bottomed chair and hurried down the hall and outdoors. Dr. Carlson had already arrived. He was scooping Grandma out of the rear seat and into his arms. She seemed very small. Uncle Packer slipped the chair under her body. "Upsy-daisy," he said, and the two men lifted the chair between them.

Sally closed the car door. She needed something else to do to prove how caring and helpful she could be. When Dr. Carlson and Uncle Packer went into the house, she followed and removed the iron that held the door. She watched them ease the chair with Grandma around the corner into the bedroom hall. She stared, fascinated, horrified. Water was dripping down the seat of the chair. No, it was dripping down Grandma's percale skirt. Urine? Sally felt her gorge rise and swallowed a lump of terror in her throat. She ran pell-mell down the porch step between the pillars and over the lawn. She fled across the field and into the Pine Grove, and flung herself headlong into the hammock.

Grandma was not sick. She was *not*. She couldn't be. The idea of Grandma being really sick was impossible. Sally made fists of her hands against the musty canvas. She was aware of a trembly new feeling, something akin to apprehension, but with a different strand to it. Sally sat up. She did not know what to do. Perhaps someone would call her from the house. She waited.

CHAPTER X

And waited and waited. There seemed to be no move-
ment at the windows of Grandma's room. Aunt Samantha came home and went into the house. Dr. Carlson
came out with his black satchel and drove away. Neither
Uncle Packer nor Aunt Samantha appeared. No one
called Sally from the house. Everyone had forgotten
about her, she thought.

Instead: "Sal-leeee!" It was Evie, jogging toward the
Grove. Sally had never been so glad to see anyone in her
life. Evie was part of the Everyday; she was brash and
normal and lively. If Sally did not mention Grandma's
strange illness, Evie would of course assume Grandma
was in the house bristling around as usual.

So when Evie, panting, stood before the hammock
and said, "I brought some *noshes*—things to eat, you

know." Sally said nothing. She peered into the paper bag Evie held out and smelled a delightful aroma of almonds and vanilla.

"Take one," said Evie. "Aunt Lou came to visit. She always brings food. She thinks you can't eat right in the country." Sally helped herself to a macaroon with coconut curls. It was delicious.

Evie took one and said, "Have another. We got lots." Holding the bag, Evie plopped down beside Sally in the hammock. Evie was solid and made the canvas bounce as if it were on springs.

"Hey, that's fun," said Evie. She stood and dropped into the hammock again. Sally vibrated like a bowl of Jell-O and had to giggle. "You do it for me," said Evie.

They took turns, plummeting into the canvas so hard they threw each other about. Finally, they sprawled exhausted on the pine needles and finished the crumbs in the pastry bag.

It seemed very late. Slide Mountain had turned purple as the sun went down. Evie said, "I better go home for dinner." She tried to retie her bow which hung, frazzled, at one side. "Come have dinner with me, Sally. Can you?"

Sally's anxiety, thinly covered by Evie's game, returned full tilt. What about Grandma? She did not want to sit at the table with Grandma's chair empty and know Grandma was sick in bed. She was even reluctant to go into the house and find out what was happening.

But she said, "I'll go ask." She dragged her feet up the sun-porch steps and stood in the kitchen. Nobody was cooking anything. She heard muffled voices down the hall in Grandm's room. Sally did not want to go down there. She wrote on the grocery pad beside the sink: "I am having dinner with Evie at the hotel. Sally." She closed the door with great care behind her.

She returned to Evie, who waited at the bottom of the rear steps. "Okay?" said Evie. Sally only nodded. As they reached Grossman's, Evie said, "Listen. You got to show my Aunt Lou how you curtsey. Too bad you got those pants on. Do it anyway, huh?"

Sally felt foolish, but she curtsied when she was introduced to Aunt Lou. "Very nice," said Aunt Lou, and went back to talking with Mrs. Grauber and two other women. Sally wondered where an uncle might be, or Evie's father. Perhaps they had stayed in the city. She turned away and bumped into someone close at her elbow.

"Excuse me," she said, before she realized it was a boy, not another adult.

The boy was red-haired and freckled, older than Sally by a year or two probably. "Meet my cousin, Irving," said Evie.

"How do you do?" said Sally.

But Irving stared at her, then grabbed at his shirt front. "Ahhhh-h-h-h!" he said. What was the matter with him? "Struck!" was what he said, and he fell to the floor

104

in a jumble of bony arms and legs.

"*Dummkopf*," said Evie. "What do you think you're doing?"

"I'm falling in love," said Irving. "Can't you see? I am *falling*. Gerund. Past tense: I *fell*." He closed one eye and squinted up at Sally from the carpet. "Are those beeyootiful legs I see before me?" He sprang up, grabbed her hand, and pretended to kiss her arm from wrist to elbow. Sally was not going to be made fun of by a gangling idiot. She stepped away, and this time dropped her deepest curtsey to Irving. She'd fix him with cool elegance. Her head bent almost to her knee. One braid swept the floor.

"Aargh. I'm dying, believe me." Irving knelt on the floor, but his mother pulled him up by a lock of his hair.

Mrs. Grauber laughed. "You have real aplomb, Sally." She put her arm through Sally's as if they were old, old friends. The dress she wore this evening was a marvel of chiffon in many-colored squares. Scarves of it crossed at her throat and curved over her shoulders. Sally was sorry she had to sit at the children's table with Irving and Evie and others. She had wanted to watch the delicate way the chiffon moved when Mrs. Grauber touched her napkin to her lips.

The dining room was very full, and the children's table quite noisy. Irving had rushed to sit beside her, and now he almost breathed down her neck. "Look at me," he said. "I'm talking to you, and you're not paying

105

attention. If you're going to be my girl friend, you got to pay attention to your master's voice."

"Look who's talking," said Evie. "Why would she want a *meshuggane* boyfriend like you?"

"Because I'm going to teach her how to play chess," said Irving. "You want me to teach you how, okay, Sally?" He nodded his head up and down. "Trust me. Say yes."

Sally saw Mrs. Grauber rise from the table. The chiffon dress and its scarves floated around her. "I wonder if a queen wears clothes like that," she said.

Evie hooted. "Who . . . like my *mother*? You're another goop like Irving. What a dopey couple you'll make."

But Irving cocked a sandy eyebrow at Sally and leaned toward her again. "You know what? You're different. You think a lot, don't you? You have a creative imagination." Evie gave him her horselaugh. "Come on, Sally," Irving said. "When you're finished, I am going to walk you home." He rested an arm on the back of her chair.

"No, you aren't," said Evie. "Sally's *my* friend, and *I'm* walking up the hill with her, picklepuss."

Irving threw a roll at her. Evie ducked and the roll scooted across the carpet and hit Aunt Lou's foot. That took care of *him*. Aunt Lou sailed over to the children's table. "A little clowning goes a long way," she said to Irving. "Sally can go home without anybody's help. Hurry home, Sally, it's getting dark already." Sally knew

106

when she was being rushed. She thanked the grown-ups and left. She was pretty sure Aunt Lou did not like her.

She started up Clemens Hill. A car slammed on its brakes at the curb beside her. She jumped. Aunt Samantha pushed the car door open. "Sally Moffat! Where *have* you been?"

Uh-oh.

"Get in, get in. Here I have your grandmother to worry about, and then you run off without a by-your-leave." Aunt Samantha shifted gears so sharply that the car leaped forward. "Grandma's had a stroke. Why didn't you tell us where you were going?"

"I did tell," said Sally, but she knew she was guilty. "I wrote a note on the grocery list."

"That's no place to leave a note in emergencies." Aunt Samantha was snappish. "I never look at a grocery list till morning."

From the brightness of the hotel to angry Aunt Samantha was a crashing drop. At Grossman's, she had dined in style with waitresses changing plates and forks for her. The elegant Mrs. Grauber had welcomed her and linked arms with her. Aunt Samantha did not have to yell like that! Sally sat stiff as a ramrod beside her and said nothing more.

She allowed herself to be hustled into the house. In the living room, she was confronted by a stranger in a white uniform so starched she rustled standing still. The woman said, "Found your runaway, did you?"

107

Runaway! Sally hated the woman instantly.

"This is Nurse Myers," said Aunt Samantha. "She's come to take care of Grandma tonight."

"Had your auntie real worried," said the nurse. Her voice was raspy. "Little girruls should ask before they leave." Nurse Myers showed long yellow teeth when she smiled. "Want to see grandmother? Come along, dearie, and see our nice old lady."

"No!" exclaimed Sally. She meant No, don't call Grandma a Nice Old Lady as if she were just a body in a bed. "No," Sally said again and shrank toward the stairs.

Keeping shocked eyes on Sally, Aunt Samantha groped for a chair. "Don't you care enough about your grandmother to see how she is?"

"Yes, but—" Sally did not know how to say she did not want to see Grandma in front of the nurse. In fact, she *hated* the idea of Nurse Myers touching Grandma. "What is a stroke, please?"

"Cool as a cucumber," said Aunt Samantha. How little she knew! Sally's panic was close to the surface, but she did not want to give way to her feelings in front of this unsympathetic stranger.

Nurse Myers answered, "Your grandma is paralyzed on one side. We don't know yet whether she can talk or how her brain is affected." Oh, Grandma! "Come along, Sarah. If your grandmother recognizes you, it will be an encouraging sign."

And if she *doesn't?* thought Sally. What will that mean? Miserable, and keeping her voice gruff so it

108

would not break, she said, "I think I'd rather see her in the morning." Dear God, she prayed, get Grandma well by tomorrow.

Aunt Samantha sighed. "As you like, Sally. You'll have to be quiet in the morning so Miss Myers can sleep. She's in the other room upstairs." Ugh, so she had to share her part of the cottage too.

"Hi, girlie, I thought I heard you." Uncle Packer bumbled in from the hall. His thin hair was rumpled, and his tie off. His green sleeve garters showed above his shirt elbows. "Worried about you, girlie," said Uncle Packer. "You all right?" He put his arm around Sally's shoulders.

Sally turned into his protective arms and sobbed buckets. Her tears covered her cheeks and dripped off her chin. It felt so good to be able to cry. "There, there," Uncle Packer said again and again. He patted her shoulders.

However, Aunt Samantha clucked her tongue. "There's nothing to *cry* about."

"Aw, now, Samantha," said Uncle Packer. He gave Sally another hug, but Sally was already disgusted with herself for crying like a baby, and in front of everyone. She dashed the tears away with her hands and stalked up the stairs to her room. She wished she could move in with the Graubers at the Mountain House Hotel, where everything sparkled, and people were lively, and nobody ever got sick.

CHAPter xi

At breakfast Sally shared the table with Nurse Myers, who sat in Grandma's place. The nurse also read the funnies, which were Sally's part of the morning paper. She smoked a cigarette and coughed while she read. When she had a half inch of cigarette ready to burn her fingers, she doused it in the coffee spilled in her saucer. Sally gulped with distress. The idea of *her* helping Grandma was so terrible that she had to swipe at her eyes with her napkin.

"Cinnamon toast?" said Aunt Samantha.

"No thanks. I'm not hungry." Sally escaped to the living room. She stopped by the Arctic owl and stooped to lay her head against his velvety breast. She stroked one yellow claw. *He* had not changed. Yesterday everything had been so normal; no, it had been wonderful.

110

Grandma had sat by the rock at Stone Bridge. Only yesterday!

Nurse Myers entered on her spongy shoes. "Some old buzzard he is," she said of the owl. "Run along outside, Sarah. Children need fresh air." Like an old buzzard *she* is, thought Sally.

She hesitated. She did not have to take directions from this nurse. She started to slip toward Grandma's room, but Miss Myers heard her. "The old lady's asleep. Let her rest, Sarah."

Wait till that nurse is asleep, thought Sally. She went outside, scuffed morosely in the drive, and then wandered down to the road.

"Hoopla-hoopla-watch-me-no-hands!" Cousin Irving zoomed by on a black bike. He swerved dangerously and stopped in front of Sally. He was breathing hard from pedaling up Clemens Hill. "Glad to see me?"

Sally grinned, relieved to have company. Irving was crazy but nice. "Where's Evie?" she asked.

Irving pointed downhill with his thumb but kept his eyes on Sally. "She's coming. She stopped by the iceman. That kid, she's always ready to stuff her face."

"I like ice too," said Sally. "Let's get some when the iceman stops at Aunt Samantha's." In hot weather they got a fifty-pound chunk twice a week.

"A-a-nh," said Irving. "It's just *ice*. You'd rather have a ride with me. Dare you to ride on my handlebars. Double dare." Irving rolled his bike forward until the front

111

wheel touched the toe of Sally's sneaker. He lowered his voice. "You like me a little bit, don't you?"

Maybe she did, and maybe she didn't. Sally said, as a distraction, "Here's the ice truck." The van, LINDSAY'S ICE, turned into the Meads' driveway. Behind it, red faced, pumping hard, came Evie on the blue bike. In her striped red shorts, yellow blouse, and matching red-and-yellow bow, she looked like a marigold in Grandma's garden.

Evie had to yell over the roar of the truck's noisy motor. "He said he'd give me some ice when he stops here." She and Irving left their bikes at the curb, and the three of them ran down the drive to crowd around the open tailgate. Mr. Lindsay threw aside a sawdust-covered tarp and chopped into a block of ice. Large slivers thunked along the floorboards toward them. They scooped up as much as they could jiggle from hand to hand. It was so magnificently cold!

"Thanks, mister," said Evie. "Oooo, that's a lot." Sally found a handkerchief to wrap her ice in and went back to the curb to suck on it.

"My teeth ache," said Irving. "That's enough of that stuff. How about that ride on my handlebars, Sally?" He stood up. "You ready?"

"That's too dangerous," said Evie. "Sally doesn't want to do that."

"What else is there to do around this burg?" asked Irving. He stuck his wet hands into his pockets to warm them.

"We could go see the Blodgetts' horses," said Sally. "They keep two in the field down the road."

"Nah! Horses!" Irving screwed up his face. "I'm allergic to animals. Cats, dogs, horses, *pfui!*" He pedaled his bicycle down the road, then put his feet on the handlebars. For a moment he teetered, on the brink of disaster, while Sally and Evie watched his performance from the curb.

"What's allergic?" Sally asked. She put her damp handkerchief in her bloomers pocket. It was a cool wad against her stomach.

"Like hay fever," said Evie. "His nose runs, and stuff makes him cough and sneeze. He swells up and gets blotchy over feathers and fur. Dust too, I think. I forget."

"You going to sit there all day?" Irving hollered. "This is some hick town."

"I know," said Evie. "We'll take you to the Pine Grove. Bet you've never even seen a hammock. Sally and I had an awful lot of fun in it yesterday. We bounced each other out on the ground and everything."

Irving dropped his bike at the curb and followed the two girls over the field to the Grove. "Watch," said Evie. "This is so hilarious." She dropped into the canvas. Sally dropped beside her. They jounced around, but it was not as much fun as it had been before.

Irving said, "That's just dumb."

"Okay," said Evie. "Let's give him the works. Get in,

113

Irving, and I bet we can swing you so high you fall out."

Irving stretched out in the hammock and pulled the canvas around him until only a lock of red hair showed. "You can't do it," he said, voice muffled. "I guarantee I will not be precipitated."

Behind her glasses Evie's eyes gleamed. "Bet your dessert at lunch if we do, Mr. Smarty-Pants. Swing as hard as you can, Sally." They swung the hammock until the ropes creaked and twisted. Irving lay rigid like an Egyptian mummy encased in plaster. They flopped him over twice, but he stayed in as if glued.

"My arms ache," said Sally. "Let's quit before the ropes break."

But all at once Irving sneezed so violently that his elbows jerked out of the hammock, and he had to let go. With one swift heave Evie sprawled him into the pine needles. "*OOF. No fair. Kerchoo, kerchoo.*" Irving sat up and sneezed some more. The swinging hammock came to rest with its folds upon his head. Evie laughed until she had to sit down.

"It's my allergies," said Irving. He batted the hammock and sneezed. "This danged thing's full of dust." He got to his feet. "Dang dust," he said and went to his bike.

"Oh boy," said Evie, gasping. "See what I mean about allergies?"

Sally stopped the swaying hammock. "It never makes

114

me sneeze." She walked to where Irving was coughing and hiccuping beside his bike. His nose was red and his eyes were swollen and teary. Though he tried to square his shoulders and take deep breaths, his chin twitched with hiccups. Sally's heart went out to him. She said, "Do you still want me to ride on your handlebars?"

"*Hiccup. Hic.*" Irving wiped his nose. "You mean it? You're not scared?" Sally bit her lip but shook her head. "Say, that's prime! You'll love this." Irving held the bike steady, so Sally could balance her hips on the handlebars. Her long legs dangled on either side of the front wheel.

Irving's breath was on her neck. "This'll be a real whizbang. Don't worry—that's only a metaphor." Sally's toes were cold inside her sneakers. "Hang on," Irving yelled. "Hoopla-hoopla!"

They were off like a Fourth of July rocket down Clemens Hill. The wind ripped one of Sally's braids loose, and the flurry of hair whipped across both their faces. Inches ahead of them, the orange cat with the question-mark tail sprang out of their way, and a pebble spun from under the front tire. It was a race with the wind, no brakes and intoxicating speed, until Irving skidded them to a whirling stop at the corner. He had to clasp Sally around the middle to keep her from falling headlong. "Wow," Irving said. Sally's knees felt as if they were made of water.

Evie drew up her bike beside them. "Why did you ride that crazy way? You nuts or something?"

Irving's arm was like an iron band at Sally's waist. His voice was admiring, and his hiccups were gone. "Sally, you're a whingdinger. I thought you'd be too scared to ride."

Evie said, "She *was* scared. It's just she never shows it. Not like me."

"Well, I *think* it," said Sally. "I think lots of things sometimes that I don't talk about." She was feeling very close to Evie and Irving, and she needed to admit what troubled her most. "Right now I'm scared for my grandmother. I didn't tell you before. She's sick. I have to go home and see how she is."

"Is she *very* sick?" asked Evie.

Irving was watching. His interest made her feel very brave. Sally said out loud for the first time, "Yes. She's had a stroke."

"You must be so worried," said Evie. "I'll come home with you. Maybe I can help at your house."

"I'll come also," said Irving. "I can ride fast to the drugstore if anyone has to go for medicine. I'm very reliable, you know." He wiggled his ears at Sally to cheer her up. Together he and Evie pushed their bikes and walked Sally to the crest of Clemens Hill.

"You can leave now," Evie said to her cousin. He crossed his eyes at her, but she was firm. "They don't need a lot of kids hanging around an invalid. You go tell Mama I'm staying with Sally and getting her lunch, and I'll be home later."

"Nyah," said Irving. "Well. Remember, Sally, I'm

116

going to teach you how to play chess. It's a good idea because chess is a quiet game for sick people. Maybe your grandmother wants to learn too. Let me know, huh?" He pedaled back over the hill and disappeared.

CHApter xii

Evie propped her bike by the garage, and the two girls climbed the steps to the sun porch. Aunt Samantha opened the screen door and put a finger to her lips. "Remember, Nurse Myers is asleep. Hello, Evie."

Evie whispered, "We've come to help you take care of Sally's grandmother. I could make Mrs. Byrd lunch on a tray?"

"Oh, lunch," said Aunt Samantha. She laid a finger along one cheek. "Mother's not eating yet, but there's Sally of course. I usually eat lunch in town."

"I make good tuna-fish sandwiches, Mrs. Mead," Evie said. "Can we stay with Sally's grandmother while you go to town?"

Sally wished she had thought to offer that. Evie had

good ideas. "Wellll," said Aunt Samantha.

Evie did not wait for any more of an answer than that. She found the pantry. "You got any tuna? Are there hard-boiled eggs? Where are the onions?" There was a sound of tins falling and paper bags rattling. The icebox door opened and shut with a hollow thunk that made the milk bottles clink.

"Well," said Aunt Samantha a second time. "Packer is downtown, but he's coming home at two, he said. If you can fix your own lunches . . . I'll run down to look in at the shop."

Evie came out of the pantry with her arms full. "Bring the bread," she said to Sally. "I don't want to drop the milk. These eggs got H's on them. Does that mean hard-boiled?" Sally nodded. Grandma kept a few eggs boiled in case of picnics. The two eggs Evie had were penciled with Grandma's wavery H. Grandma was such a good provider, Sally thought.

Aunt Samantha was amused by Evie. "Well organized, I see. All right, girls. If you have the slightest need for help, wake Miss Myers. Look in on Grandma. You hear, Sally? Evie's the chef, but you're responsible."

Sally set the kitchen table. She reached for her napkin in its silver ring. She needed a fresh napkin for Evie and went to the sideboard in the dining room to get one.

When she returned, Evie was mashing up egg and tuna with a dollop of mayonnaise. She asked, "How did your Grandma get sick?"

Sally said, "We went to Stone Bridge yesterday for a

picnic. Grandma fell asleep on the way home, and I don't think she's been awake since."

"It happens," said Evie.

Sally creased Evie's napkin to a triangle, then folded it over again till it was small in her hand. She twisted it as she talked. "She—I think she—looked so white in the back of the car. Something gave out, kind of, I think."

"Here," said Evie. "You'll feel better when you eat."

Evie spread the tuna salad thick onto slices of bread and cut the sandwiches. Sally bit into hers. It was rich with chopped eggs and chunks of onion. Evie was right. Even Sally's legs had been hollow with hunger. She'd been almost faint without knowing it. "You get so empty, you can't think straight, right?" Evie said.

"Ummmm." Sally chewed and swallowed. Her mother never made tuna salad this good. She frowned. "You think maybe that's what happened to me yesterday?" she said.

"*What* happened yesterday?" said Evie.

Sally wound her feet into the rungs of the stool she was sitting on. This was going to sound peculiar, but she wanted to tell Evie about her island. "I went wading up the creek, the Caspar Kill that is, and my feet got awful cold so I climbed up on a rock to get warm."

"Was your grandma there?"

"She was way back with the lunch, on the bank, getting it ready. Anyway, I sort of lay down, because it was so nice in the sun. I closed my eyes and lay there."

"So?"

"*Something* was *there*. I mean, I could feel—this big hand, overhead. I froze. Honest. I didn't dare open my eyes to see what it was, but I *felt* it, Evie. I could tell its shadow blotted out the sun for a second, and I was cold. And then you know what happened? The rock I was lying on *moved*."

Evie had stopped eating. She and Sally stared at one another. Evie whispered, "What do you think it was?"

Sally found she was whispering too. "I don't know." She paused, then put her crusts on her plate and watched her fingers crumble them.

Evie said in the same low voice, "It was a message."

"I . . . I don't know. I wondered. When Grandma got sick, and everything, I wondered if, if . . ."

"It was a warning, like," said Evie. "To watch out and take special care of your Grandma, because *she's* so special, you know what I mean?"

"Oh, yes!" said Sally. She jumped up. "I think I'll go see if Grandma's awake."

"Me too," said Evie.

Sally led the way down the bedroom hallway to Grandma's room. They tiptoed to stand inside the threshold. The curtains were pulled, so the room was dim. In the half-light, Grandma seemed as frail as a flower stalk under the covers. Her curled-up hand outside on the quilt reminded Sally how much Grandma had done with her hands. Rolled piecrust. Picked huckleberries. Opened her little tins of ginger. Sally said, in a low tone, "Grandma is funny, how she loves ginger. We'll have some when she gets well."

Evie pursed her lips, very solemn. "If she gets well."

Sally pulled Evie from the room. "What do you mean *if* she gets well?" she said fiercely. "Of *course* she'll get well."

"Don't get so mad," said Evie. "I didn't mean to scare you. It's only, well, she's awful old to be sick." She edged off down the hall. "Can we look at some of your aunt's things?"

Sally took a deep breath to slow her racing heart. "I'll show you the owl," she said. They entered the living room. "Feel how soft he is."

Evie ruffled the owl's feathers and pinged his sharp beak with her fingernail. "That's how mad you just looked," she said. She turned toward the mermaid piano. "That is really something. How does it sound?"

"We can't play it while that nurse is asleep," said Sally.

"I've never been anywhere but the kitchen before," said Evie. "Can I see your room?" They slipped quietly up the stairs. Nurse Myers' door, on the landing opposite Sally's, was closed.

"Tell you what," said Sally. "We better go in the Fort to talk, so we don't wake *her*." With only a momentary twinge at revealing the secret place to Evie, Sally unlatched the door in the wall.

Evie glanced around the shelves, at the box kite, the stools, and the old piece of carpet. "It's so nice. Why do you call it a Fort? It's part of the attic, isn't it?"

"My brothers always call places forts," said Sally. "They make forts under their beds or the dining-room table or behind the couch. Here they pretended that the nails coming through from the shingles were Indian arrowheads."

"It's like being on the inside of a porcupine," Evie said. She moved away from the ceiling as if the points might stick her. She examined Sally's treasures, the agate marbles Sam had left, the deer, the milkweed pods. "What's this heap? Rocks? They're pretty."

"I collected them yesterday at Stone Bridge. Here's one Grandma said was a friendstone. You can hold it so it fits your thumb." Sally turned over the stone so Evie saw how her thumb slipped in and out.

"Let *me*," said Evie. A blissful look came into her gray eyes. "Isn't that ni-ice. I bet it *is* a friendstone like your grandma said. Can I have it? I'm your friend."

"Uh-uh," said Sally.

Evie was not disturbed at all. "Okay. You don't have to give me everything I ask for. It's a habit I got. It only means like something."

Yes, Sally had thought so. Evie asked for things out of admiration. It was just her way.

Evie reached up to her hairbow. "I'll leave you my bow, so you'll have something to remember me by next summer." She unpinned the clip and hair fell over her glasses.

"Why? You'll be here too, won't you?" said Sally, as

122

she slid her thumb in and out of the friendstone.

"Probably not," said Evie. "My mother likes to go somewhere different each year. Probably we'll never come here again, or not for a long time." She balanced the bow in its clip on the middle shelf.

Never come again! And Evie seemed so calm about it. By contrast, Sally saw her own life in a rut that ran from same house to same old school. Same neighbors. Same trees. Same sidewalks so familiar that Sally could step over the cracks blindfolded. Their vacation at the lake her father liked to fish in was the same every July. Wistfully, Sally said, "I wonder if I'd like that? Every year someplace different."

"That's nothing," said Evie. "We change apartments every couple years because Mama likes to redecorate. I don't care much. Except I have to keep finding new friends." She touched the stone under Sally's thumb. "Maybe you could put the friendstone in your grandma's hand, the one that was outside the covers. Maybe it'd make her feel better."

"Yes!" Evie had noticed the emptiness too and how it did not seem right for Grandma's hand to be curled around nothing but thin air. They left the Fort, stifled giggles as they passed Nurse Myers' door, and tiptoed into Grandma's room. Grandma had moved and lay on her back, but her eyes were still shut. Her silvery hair was rumpled against the bolster. Sally longed to brush out the curls. She must do that later.

Evie nudged her and whispered, "Put it in her hand.

It will fit right." Sally slipped the friendstone, warm from her own palm, inside Grandma's half-opened right hand.

Grandma's hand tightened around the stone. She opened her eyes—blue, blue eyes that gazed up at the two of them. Sally said, "It's the friendstone, Grandma, the one you said would mean I always had a friend." Grandma smiled a crooked smile, but her eyes spoke love. "I'm so glad you're feeling better, Grandma," said Sally.

There was a creak in the ceiling overhead. The upstairs lavatory flushed, and water gurgled through wall pipes. "Your nurse is coming, Mrs. Byrd," said Evie.

Sally's stomach contracted. She did not want to see her grandmother with Nurse Myers there, plumping up the bolster or giving her a pill. "Grandma, I have to go now." She stroked Grandma's knuckles around the friendstone, then pushed Evie out the door.

Evie blew a kiss toward the bed. In the hall, she said, "Why do you leave her, now she's awake?"

"That awful nurse is coming," muttered Sally. "I don't want to be in there when *she* is." There was a squeak of rubber soles on the stairway. "In here," Sally whispered, and pushed Evie through the doorway of Aunt Samantha and Uncle Packer's bedroom. They hid inside and waited.

They could hear Nurse Myers walking into Grandma's room. "How is my dear old lady this afternoon?" she

124

said loudly, but there was no audible reply from Grandma.

"If it were me, I'd spit in her eye," Sally growled.

Evie was restless. She glanced around the bedroom at the two spool beds and the rag carpets Grandma had sewn long ago. She sat on Uncle Packer's bed and tested the springs. "If we can't talk to your Grandma," she said, "what'll we do now?"

CHAPTER XIII

"Wait a minute till that old nurse goes away," said Sally. She could hear the shades go up and then the windows being raised. "She's a regular demon for fresh air."

Evie jounced higher on the bed. "Do your aunt and uncle sleep here?"

"Yes." Sally listened for the nurse to leave, but a chair grated across the floor. Maybe Nurse Myers was going to sit awhile.

"Let's try on their clothes," said Evie. She threw open a closet door. On the top shelf was Aunt Samantha's best red-and-black straw hat. Evie poked the hat off with a furled umbrella.

Sally was doubtful. "We ought to ask first."

"There you go," said Evie. "Your aunt won't mind. My mother doesn't. Remember what fun we had trying on *my* clothes?" She put the hat on her head and admired the way the roses vibrated in the mirror. "What do you think?" she said. She placed her hands on her hips and wiggled them. "Hot stuff, huh? Will you have jam in your tea, Mrs. Minsky?"

Sally flung open Uncle Packer's closet. He must be wearing his new panama downtown, but his winter derby was in a box. Sally settled it on the back of her head, the way she wore her Sunday sailor hat to church.

"You got no style." Evie tipped the hat over Sally's right eye. "That's it. That's the way dancers wear them when they do an act at the Roxy."

Sally saw herself in the long mirror. There was a dashing figure in there, cool but impudent. "I ought to have a cane," she said. "They had canes in the vaudeville I saw on my birthday."

Evie rummaged in the closet and came out with a cane. "Here. I'll show you how to do a turn." She linked arms with Sally and showed her how to shuffle and bend, one foot forward and back, the other foot forward and back. "Yes, sir, that's my baby," she sang.

"Sssshh." Sally collapsed on a bed. "You're so funny, but we got to be quieter. We don't want Nurse Myers to hear us."

Evie straightened her glasses. The hat had pushed them askew. "Myers-schmyers," she said, but she stopped singing.

"*I* know," said Sally. "That hat needs the fur piece."

127

She climbed up on a chair to explore higher in Aunt Samantha's closet. She drew out a rope of little animal skins from folds of tissue and mounds of moth flakes and handed it to Evie. There were pointed, whiskery noses and glittery black eyes. A tail drooped behind Evie's back.

"Irving would sneeze his head off at this." Evie arranged the whiskers under her chin. "It tickles."

Sally put on her uncle's green velvet smoking jacket, which hung to her knees. Flapping the long sleeves over her hands, she capered around the room. Evie kicked off her sandals and hopped on a bed. When she tried to do a hula, Sally attempted a cancan. They leaped from bed to bed, passing each other in midair. "Watch me," commanded Sally, and she kicked a pillow as if it were a football.

"Girls, girls!" Nurse Myers was in the doorway. "Get off those beds!" Sally, horrified, stopped jumping immediately. Evie peered at Nurse Myers between flopping roses. "You," rasped Miss Myers. "Here is Sally's grandmother just passed away, poor soul, and you're in here acting like clowns. I have to call the doctor and the family. Put those clothes back where you found them." Nurse Myers turned like a general and left.

Sally removed the derby and placed it in its box. She hung the smoking jacket and cane in the closet. Her heart, frozen to ice, lay somewhere, unmeltable, in her stomach instead of in her chest. Still on the bed, Evie said, "She smiled at us, your grandmother. When you put the friendstone in her hand, she smiled. How can that old nurse mean she's *dead*? How does she *know*?"

"She's a nurse," said Sally. "She's supposed to know." Sally felt like two people. She watched herself from afar. She believed Nurse Myers, and she didn't believe her. Because you could not believe the incomprehensible. The sun shone too brightly outdoors for anyone to die.

"Ssssh," siad Evie. "She's on the phone. Listen."

"Tell Dr. Carlson I checked her when I came downstairs, and when I came back from putting the kettle on, she was gone. . . . Slept away. . . . Yes. As soon as he can then." They heard the click of the receiver. Then it ticked again. Nurse Myers now spoke to the Operator, who sat at her switchboard in downtown Cottersville. "Give me ten seventy-eight J."

"She's calling the shop. Aunt Samantha," whispered Sally.

"Let's go see your grandma," said Evie, "while *she's* on the phone."

They went. "Sally's grandmother," said Evie. "Mrs. Byrd, wake up. Wake up." Evie leaned over and jiggled the headboard.

"Don't" said Sally. Grandma lay on her back. Her hand still had the friendstone in it. It was strange, but Sally could see that the stone was no longer *held*. It only rested there. Slept away, Nurse Myers had said. Slipped away on business of her own—that would be more like Grandma. Sally did not at once feel sad, but tears spilled over her cheeks.

"Oy vay," said Evie. Tears of sympathy steamed her glasses. Together the two left the room and wandered to the kitchen.

Nurse Myers found them there. For once she sounded almost gentle. "It's no doubt for the best, Sarah dear," she said. And to Evie, "I think, little girl, that you should run along home now. Watch the stairs." She held the door open as Evie, half blinded with tears, wiped her nose on her blouse sleeve and turned to go.

Nurse Myers closed the screen door behind her so it did not bang. She said, "Your auntie will be home directly."

Sally went into the sun porch and sat in the chair where Grandma had sat just a few days ago, bathing her eyes that were old and tired. She smoothed the cushion. Grandma was so light that she never left a dent in a pillow or disturbed the nap on a rug when she walked. Sally could not stay still. The emptiness in the house made an ache in her insides. Her own body seemed a husk, dried out, without sap, blood, or emotion. Her tears had dried when Evie left. Sally covered her face with her hands and took deep, sobbing breaths.

Her body grieved, but her mind was unaccepting. Grandma could not possibly be dead. That old nurse was wrong, wrong. But she had seen Grandma's lifeless hand. Oh God. God, make Grandma alive. You could do it if You really wanted to. *I need Grandma*, Sally

130

thought. You can't take her away from me now. She was desperate, almost angry. She rubbed her dry cheeks and then socked the hassock. *Whack*. Dust motes flew crazily into the sunshine. The whole world was against her. The universe was wrong. It had removed Grandma by mistake. "G-g-grandm-m-ma!" she called, feeling as though grief would wrench her heart right out of her aching body.

She could not sit on the sun porch. She went down the back steps and crossed the field to the Pine Grove. She leaned into the musty canvas of the hammock. Finally, in salty streams that washed over her lips, tears fell. Awash in the agony of her own weeping, Sally heard a light, calm voice sift down between the pine boughs: "All right, all right," it said. Sally closed her eyes, as if Grandma's knotty knuckled hands had stroked the lids. A breeze dried her face. Then she knew it was true. Her grandmother had gone away and left her behind.

CHAPTER XIV

The next morning Sally went out to the front step to finish her breakfast muffin. It was too upsetting to eat in the kitchen, and Aunt Samantha seemed to understand her need not to see Grandma's empty chair. Sally had brushed, combed, and braided her hair, dressed in a clean blouse and skirt and her new sandals, but as she leaned against the white pillar, she did not know why. She did not know the why of anything.

The household had been very busy since yesterday afternoon. The undertaker's men had come for Grandma. Neighbors had come by with covered pots of food and words of comfort. Uncle Packer had ordered folding chairs from a West Kill caterer, because services were to be in the Meads' living room. The piano had already been shoved against one wall, and the owl had been taken to the sun porch. The funeral was tomorrow, to give relatives a chance to come from Albany. The ones in Texas and Oregon had wired but were not making the trip. Sally had observed, or been told, all this, but nothing seemed important.

Her father was due by lunchtime today. Her mother and Sam and Colin were not coming. Both the boys were still coughing; and besides, her parents thought they were too young for a funeral. Sally herself had never been to a funeral and hardly knew what was expected of her. The one thing she was sure of was that she had seldom felt so useless. She crumbled a crust of muffin and threw the bits on the lawn. They lay there; there weren't any finches this morning. Sally sighed. She got up from the steps and went to the side of the house where the flowers grew in neat rows to catch the early sun.

Evie found her wandering between the sweetpeas that Grandma had staked out. "G'morning," said Evie. She stood and blinked at Sally from behind her glasses. "What are you doing?"

Sally brushed her fingertips over the purple and pink flowers. "Nothing, I guess."

"I thought I'd come sit *shiva* with you. If that's all right."

"Sit shiva?"

"Jews sit shiva when someone dies. The family does, with friends to help. We're supposed to mourn for seven days. That's what sitting shiva is, staying home for seven days, because shiva is Hebrew for seven. My mother said I could come sit with you."

Sally moved down the tied lengths of plants. "Sitting? I don't think I can." She had not slept well last night, tossing and turning till the sheets were wadded. She had worried and worried about their dancing and their dressing up. In the dark, it had seemed so terrible.

Evie said, "Well, it's not *sitting* exactly. We're supposed to talk about your grandma—the good things. How she was so pretty, you know, with those silver curls."

Sally swallowed. She headed out of the garden, toward the uncultivated meadow. "Grandma and I picked huckleberries way over there," she said. "You want to see the bushes?" Evie walked beside her. At the tumbledown stone wall, where Grandma had lifted her skirts to climb, Sally paused and shaded her eyes to look over the long grass.

She had to clear her throat. "Grandma liked the wild things," she said. "She seemed so—close—to the flowers and the berries and the trees, you know what I mean?"

"Yes, I think so," said Evie. "It's as if she were a part of the mountains."

Sally faced Evie squarely. "Yes. And I think she knew how children have to grow. They can't be fussed at all the time. They have to be shown, not *told* every minute of their lives." Sally appreciated how Grandma had

134

guided her, always so gentle, but with that underlying streak of granite, like the mountains, underneath.

"It's nice the way she talked," said Evie. "I liked the way her words came out soft and even."

"Me too," said Sally. "I liked her old-fashioned words, and to hear her talk about old-fashioned times. But you should have heard her the day she got mad at your father because he hit a golf ball at her hat. Did I tell you?"

Evie shook her head. Her bow, a subdued blue this morning, bobbled. "Tell about it."

"First I thought your father was angry at her for telling him off—that he had to be more careful and look out for people. Then he smiled and was all right and shook hands. What I thought was, he must have liked her speaking out like that."

Evie grinned. "My father likes people with *chutzpah*."

"What's that?"

"What your grandma had. Sometimes it means nerve, or guts to do something, maybe a gutsy kind of courage. I think your grandma was telling *you* off, in her way, the day we made the pies. Remember?"

So short a time ago! "Grandma said nobody's perfect, not grandmothers either." Sally did not know why she remembered that, of the wonderful bits to remember about Grandma. She put her chin in her hand. "I can't figure out, Evie—do you think we were *dancing* when Grandma died?"

"I suppose, well, it could be."

135

Sally gave a little moan. "It's just—how *could* I?" It seemed so heartless.

"I don't think your grandma would have minded," said Evie. "She'd've *liked* to see us have a good time. She wasn't like that starchy nurse."

Grandma *had* enjoyed liveliness. "But I hope she didn't mind if she heard us," said Sally.

"You worry over stuff that doesn't count," said Evie. "You don't have to be such a worrywart. Your grandma wasn't." Evie pulled a chip of lichen from the wall. "Do you believe your grandma's in Heaven now?"

"I—don't know." Sally clenched both hands. Hopeless, everything was so hopeless. "That's where they'll tell me she's supposed to be. I'd rather she was here." Sally's eyes brimmed and flooded. Evie handed her a fresh handkerchief. Sally scrubbed her eyes dry. The sun was rising higher, hotter, and brighter. She said, after a moment, "I wish I could *do* something. I mean, Aunt Samantha took Grandma's ginger out of her hiding places, and there isn't anything for *me* to do."

"Do you want to visit us?" said Evie. "My mother said to invite you to the hotel if you want to. She wouldn't let Irving come and bother the household, she said, but he wanted to help you sit shiva. If you visit the hotel, then he can help too. Can you come?" Evie got up and took Sally's hand.

Just moving seemed helpful. "I'll go ask," Sally said. They went in the house to find Aunt Samantha.

"Of course. Go with Evie," Aunt Samantha said.

"Moping won't bring Grandma back." She was preoccupied, planning menus and consulting the West Kill Railroad timetable. Uncle Packer had to meet several trains and had groaned he was nothing but a chauffeur. Sally noticed that both he and Aunt Samantha had a strained look around the eyes. She had a ridiculous thought—they need Grandma to help them—but caught herself before she said it out loud.

This time, Sally and Evie walked decorously down Clemens Hill. Irving met them on the road. "I been riding up and down for hours," he said. "I thought somebody might need a messenger or something." Sally was touched. He did not offer to carry her on his handlebars but got off his bike and walked with them down the hill.

At the hotel, Sally met Mrs. Grauber with several others, waiting for the limousine to drive them to the art galleries in the next valley. With a hat and gloves on, Mrs. Grauber seemed at first remote and citified. "Good morning, Sally," she said. She put her arms around Sally and kissed her on the cheek. The warmth of her hug came as a surprise. "You take care of Sally," Mrs. Grauber said to Evie and Irving. "Dear, I'm so sorry I never met your grandmother. You will miss her very much. One loses a little piece of one's heart when someone so beloved dies." She was the first adult to be so honest about grieving. Everyone else was matter-of-fact and hid their grief to protect her. Now, because Mrs. Grauber's sympathy brought her sorrow to the surface, Sally's eyes filled and spilled over.

Mrs. Grauber put one gloved finger under her chin and wiped away two tears with a scented lawn handkerchief. "So, so," she said and beckoned to Irving.

Irving took Sally's elbow and guided her to one of the side parlors that was empty. Sally felt fragile, as if she were an egg. "That's the granddaughter," said a respectful voice as they passed. Sally had seldom been regarded as someone of importance, and it gave her a solemn feeling.

"I'm going to teach you how to play chess," said Irving. "It's a quiet, mental type game." He set out a checkerboard and dumped white and black pieces on the card table beside it. "Evie's too dumb to learn. She doesn't like to listen and think. *You* do."

"Go soak your head," said Evie. "The truth is you're sweet on Sally, and you want to sit close to her." Irving's ears got red as his hair, but he only turned his shoulder to Evie. She rifled the magazine rack and sat on a sofa with her feet on the velvet.

Irving pulled two chairs side by side. "I'll show you first how the pieces move," he said to Sally. He selected a castle and a horse's head he called a knight and pressed them into Sally's right and left hands. He closed his own fingers over hers as if she might drop the pieces. His fingers were warm on her icy ones. "The knight goes up one and over two, or vice versa," he said.

Evie gave an enormous yawn. "If you're going to be

such a big bore, you could at least give us some gum," she said. Irving took a package of Blackjack from his pocket. There were only two sticks left. He broke one in half and gave the half to Evie. He extended the whole one to Sally. "Well! I like *that*," said Evie. She waved the half piece in the air at him.

"You don't have to like it," said Irving.

Evie put out a foot and hooked it around a rung of her cousin's chair. One pull and Irving was on the floor, bringing the card table, the board, and the chessmen down on top of him. It was so much like a scramble with Sam and Colin that Sally joined in. She found herself sitting in the middle of Irving's back, while Evie grabbed off his shoes and tickled his feet. Irving hollered and laughed. Evie yelled, "Itchie kitchie koo," and Sally giggled.

Evie stopped abruptly. "Oh!" She was aghast. "I forgot. Your heart is breaking for your grandma."

Sally untangled herself. Whatever was she thinking of! She went to the sofa and sat with her skirt pulled over her bare knees and her feet flat on the floor. Irving cleared his throat and righted the table. They were silent.

Evie handed him his shoes. "I'm sorry," she said. She gathered up chess pieces from the rug.

"Yes, okay," said Irving. He folded himself beside Sally on the velvet sofa, near but not touching. He became very formal. "I believe your grandmother was a great-grandmother. That's quite unusual, I think."

139

"I never knew the one of her family who was my own grandmother," said Sally. "The one who had my father, that is. I think it must be nice, though, to be a great-grandmother."

"You are very lucky," said Irving. "I don't have *any* grandmothers or grandfathers to know. They're in Germany somewhere. And France."

Irving was so sober Sally placed a finger on his wrist to comfort him. "Maybe you'll visit them someday."

"Me too," said Evie. She had relaid the chess board and drawn up the chairs, this time three of them. "Are we learning chess or not?"

"I'm ready," said Sally. She was amazed that, for a few seconds, she had been able to think of someone else besides Grandma. Sally observed, "Sitting shiva is all right, but I can't forget my grandmother after just seven days. Then what?"

"You kind of keep her here," said Evie. She placed a hand on the front pleats of her blouse, over her heart. "Mourning is for now, but remembering is forever."

CHAPTER XV

At Grandma's funeral, Sally sat between her father and Aunt Samantha in the first row of folding chairs in the living room. She was grateful to her father because he held her hand throughout the service. It was good to have him there.

Grandma was in a casket at the front of the room, under a blanket of palest pink roses. Mr. Merget, the Methodist minister, spoke of Grandma's kind and loving spirit, but the elegant box in which she lay did not seem, to Sally, to fit that loving spirit. Sally looked away, out the windows. Grandma should be out there, roaming a mountainside, pulling the burrs out of her skirt.

Mrs. Thornton, the organist from the church, played Grandma's favorite hymn, "Abide with Me," on the mermaid piano. When they all sang, "Fast falls the eventide; The darkness deepens; Lord, with me abide," Sally's

141

throat constricted. She could not finish the hymn. She was sad but strangely composed. She could not believe Grandma was under Uncle Packer's roses. When they rode to the Cottersville Cemetery behind the hearse, Sally knew that Grandma was not going to be lowered into the earth. The formality of the rows of headstones and the carefully clipped grass were not a place for Grandma to be at home. None of this was like Grandma, or becoming to her. Sally ached and ached to talk to her, or since that was not possible, at least to talk *about* her.

Now that the funeral and what they called the "interment" were over, the rest of the family talked of everything else except Grandma. Sally sat on the arm of her father's chair. She was the only child present. "Take RCA," he was explaining. "It rose over four hundred from eighty-five this past year." The important numbers, that Grandma had been eighty-two, and that she had been born in 1847, and now, in 1929, she was gone—these were not mentioned.

Sally wandered from the sun porch to the kitchen to see what Aunt Samantha was doing. She was perking coffee and setting out sugar and cream in the best silver. There was an immense ham on the dining-room table. Uncle James was in there sharpening a knife on a whetstone. He was getting ready to carve. Cousin Isabelle piled .the plates in front of him and arranged cut-glass dishes of olives and jellies. Sally recognized a dish of

Grandma's mustard pickles. She turned back to the kitchen.

Uncle Packer had gotten out little glasses and one of his illegal bottles. With a wink, he offered them to the relatives to "ward off chill." It was a warm sunny day, but Sally understood. He must mean the chill of the cemetery.

And yet all around her now it was like a party, people gabbing with one another, talking and eating, without a care for losing Grandma. That did not seem quite right either. Sally had had little breakfast, but she could not sit still to eat. In the midst of everyone's busyness, she stood in the hall, outside Grandma's closed door. The front-door buzzer went off over her head, and she started. As she suspected, no one else heard it over the general conversation. She answered the door herself.

Evie stood on the columned front porch. Her black patent leather Mary Janes were very shiny. There was a black taffeta bow in her hair. Evie touched it as if to make sure it was still there, or for Sally to notice it. When she did so, the large pastry box she was holding slid sideways. Evie righted it with both hands and extended the box to Sally. "It's for the family," she said. "My mother sent it. It's bagels she ordered. They're for funerals, the bagels. She said I should give the box to your aunt."

"Come in," said Sally. "She's in the kitchen."

Aunt Samantha, wearing her black silk dress and satin

hat, leaned by the sink to drink coffee from a cracked mug. "Hello, Evie dear," she said. "It's nice of you to come and see Sally, and us too. Is that for me?"

Evie had a speech. She sounded more formal than usual. "Mrs. Mead, my mother says how sorry she is about Sally's great-grandmother, and your mother, and she sent these bagels for the after-funeral feast." Oh, Sally thought, the party going on around her was what was expected. It was ordinary after-funeral behavior. It was not so strange if the Graubers understood it too.

Aunt Samantha cut the green cord on the box with a bread knife. The box was piled three deep with hole-in-the-middle rolls. "How kind," said Aunt Samantha. "Doughnuts."

"They're *bay-gels*. For funerals. With the cream cheese in the tinfoil. Try one." Evie cut one in half, spread cream cheese on one section, and gave it to Aunt Samantha. "Good?"

Evie sliced more bagels. Sally got a silver platter and circulated among the guests. Several times she had to explain what bagels were. It was fun to watch people's expressions as they tasted. Uncle Packer took only one bite. He complained it stuck in his false teeth. Sally returned to the kitchen, where Evie was busy slicing.

Sally's father came for more coffee and saw them together at the enamel table. He stood beside Sally for a moment. Then, "What's this—*stuff*?" he said. He gave a sliced bagel a little flip with his thumbnail.

Instantly, Sally knew what her father was thinking, as

144

clearly as if he had said it. She heard his hidden question. ". . . And what's this Jewish kid doing here? With *this* food, in *this* house, with *my* daughter?" Evie heard his tone of voice and wrinkled her forehead and did not look up at Mr. Moffat.

Sally said, "This is Evie Grauber. She's my friend from the hotel on the corner. Her mother sent the bagels."

"There's enough food around here already, enough to sink a ship," said Mr. Moffat. He pulled a watch out of the pocket of his best suit. "Time to pack, Sally. I want to get off the mountain by dark."

"Ohhhh," said Evie. "We're sitting shiva."

"What?" Mr. Moffat asked.

"I can't go home today," Sally said. "My time isn't up yet, and Uncle Packer is going to drive me home. That's what you said when I came; I'm to have three weeks, and if Ma can't come, Unce Packer'll take me home instead of you. Right now, I have to do what Evie said. I have to mourn Grandma for four more days. That's what sitting shiva means."

"Nonsense," said her father. "Change your dress, or come as you are. I want to leave in half an hour. Tell this girl you have to stop playing now so you can get ready." Her father would not speak directly to Evie. He was dismissing her as if she were a telephone Sally could simply hang up.

"No," said Sally. "Grandma and I, uh, we have been friends of Evie's. Grandma said not to carry grudges. . . . I mean—" Sally fumbled with her ideas, desperate to

145

make him understand. "She would say, if she were here, you have to have the grace to let me make up my own mind. About things and friends and everything." Her father was cold eyed. Sally clung to the thought that she stood as tall as his chin. Her father was not as big a man as she had remembered.

Aunt Samantha came to take a slice of bagel. She put some ham on it and talked around a mouthful. "You know, Penny, Packer wants to drive down the mountain next week, and he promised to take Sally then."

"But I'm here now. It's a waste for Sally not to go home with me."

Sally's eyes burned. "I don't care what you say. I am going to *stay*."

"Start packing," said her father and turned away.

Aunt Samantha unrumpled Sally's collar so it lay flat. "Penny, I would be grateful for Sally's company as long as you can spare her."

"Wellll." Mr. Moffat's upper lip rose as if it were going to sneer. He was not graceful about surrendering. "I suppose. You may be lonesome around here."

Evie tugged at Sally's belt. "Let's take bagels to the Fort," she whispered. They gathered several in a napkin and left. Inside the attic door, Sally discovered she was ravenous. She ate three bagels with cream cheese and began to feel alive. She beamed at Evie.

"Jiminy!" Evie saw the friendstone on a shelf. "Did you take it back?" Sally had placed it on a saucer printed with bluebirds. Evie picked up the stone and rubbed her thumb slowly in and out of its hollow. "It was in your Grandma's hand when she died."

"I wanted to leave it, but Nurse Myers gave it to me. I brought it up here." Sally blew a speck off the saucer. "You want it?"

Evie held the friendstone to her cheek. "You need it to remind you of your Grandma."

Without even closing her eyes, Sally had a crystal-clear picture of Grandma as she used to be. She could see Grandma thumping dough, Grandma picking a sprig of wintergreen or straightening the sunhat. Sally did not need any *thing* to remind her of Grandma. "No, I'd rather you have it," she told Evie. "Grandma said it was a friendstone, and you're my friend, even if I don't see you again for a long time. You better have it in New York."

"Thank you," said Evie. She polished the stone on her skirt. "I better go home now. Mama made me promise not to stay too long."

Sally let Evie out the front door. "I'll see you tomorrow." Irving was waiting at the curb. He and Evie both waved as they started down the hill.

Sally pushed through the crowd of people in the living room and went to the kitchen for a glass of milk. The table was littered with stacks of soiled dishes and glasses. She put the rubber plug in the sink and let hot water run. She dumped in loads of Rinso and gathered up plates to wash. Hearing the water, Cousin Isabelle came to help. "What an enterprising chick," she said and patted her shoulder. Sally smiled and answered questions politely, but her thoughts were elsewhere.

It was strange, but Evie had turned out to be a true friend. She wasn't perfect, but she knew how to be a comfort. When you *needed* her, she was there.

Nothing's perfect, that was what Grandma had said. What was important was that Grandma and Sally had loved one another, and Sally guessed, she loved Evie too, flaws and all. Hmmmp-hmmmp, Grandma would have said, with a knowing glint in her eyes. Sally had missed that little sound of Grandma's. She tested her voice with it, to the soapsuds. "Hmmmp-hmmmp," Sally said.

Aunt Samantha slopped the coffee she was pouring. "What's that?" she said.

"Nothing," said Sally, but she bent her head to hide her smile.

"I must be hearing things," Aunt Samantha said. "Overtired, I guess. I thought I heard Mother, that little noise she used to make."

You're right, thought Sally, sloshing dishes up and down. Grandma's always here. Only now, she's inside of *me*. Hmmmp-hmmmp, Sally whispered to herself.